**HELEN WALTON**

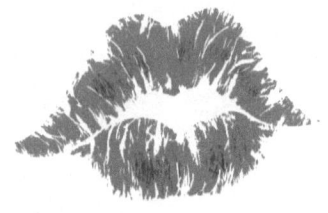

**EVERNIGHT PUBLISHING ®**

**www.evernightpublishing.com**

# LOVE NEGOTIATIONS

# HELEN WALTON

# DEDICATION

For Erica Karwoski and the goat that kicked her in the face.

# HELEN WALTON

# LOVE NEGOTIATIONS

## Billionaires' Reluctant Brides, 3

### Helen Walton

### Copyright © 2022

⋍·•·◆·•·⋍

### Chapter One

*One Month Ago*

I pressed my ear against the door listening for her footsteps. Terrible, I know. It wasn't entirely my fault. Since working as a nanny for the Burberrys, I'd become accustomed to listening to them since one of my bedroom walls backed onto theirs. They weren't quiet in the bedroom or any other place in their Los Angeles mansion they had sex. It was inevitable I'd not only hear them but see them in the act.

The first time was accidental after I'd fallen asleep in the theatre room inside the blanket fort their twin sons built, and the boys had long since gone to bed. I hadn't meant to fall asleep. Prue and Will having sex, woke me. I'd peeked through the gaps in the blankets like a Peeping Tom. Now I was a Peeping Tom whenever the opportunity presented itself. There was a desire buried deep inside me to watch other people have sex.

Even Prue and William Burberry.

Or listen to them.

Either way, watching and listening got me excited beyond anything my ex-boyfriend had ever achieved.

Prue's heels clicked down the stairs of the mansion. I eased open my bedroom door and slipped into the hallway. Her underwear-clad body disappeared from the staircase and into the downstairs hallway. I hurried down the stairs, glimpsing her thong-covered ass slipping into William's office. Prue was gorgeous. If I was into women, she'd be the type of woman I'd go for—pale skin, long black hair brushing against her lower back with every movement. I loved seeing her tresses sway when her husband screwed her. I loved seeing his body, too, firm and toned, all man.

They exhibited sex better than any porno I'd watched. And I'd watched a lot since discovering my kink.

The door closed behind Prue. I hurried down the rest of the stairs and squished my ear against the solid timber. The door was hard to hear through, but Prue's screams of pleasure were always loud enough to penetrate the wood. Ha, wood. I bet William boasted hard wood seeing his wife in her lingerie.

Voices mumbled through the door. *What was taking them so long?* I squinted at the video baby monitor in my hand, which I'd muted. The twins were toddlers now and slept through the night, but I still monitored the screen in case they needed me.

*Come on, get on with it.*

I ran a finger over my plump bottom lip. My ex-boyfriend always called my lips kissable. Whatever the hell that was supposed to mean.

The voices stopped speaking.

This was it. There was more often than not a bit

of quiet before the big show. I squished my ear harder against the door until it almost hurt. The door swung open; I stumbled into a suited chest. *Oh, crap.* Warm hands grabbed my shoulders, keeping me upright. I left my face buried in his chest, too mortified to acknowledge William caught me eavesdropping. I couldn't glance up. Embarrassing heat filled my face. My boss would realize that I listened to them have sex. The door snicked shut.

*Don't look up. Don't look up.*

If the kids woke on the monitor in my hand right now, it would be the one thing to save me from losing my job.

A firm hand tipped my chin up. My gaze met the sparkling gray steel eyes of Marco Lawrence, best friend of William, surrogate uncle to the twins, and the hottest forty-year-old man I'd ever known. Forty-three, to be exact. I opened my mouth to deny what it looked like, but he placed his finger over my lips.

The scent of his masculine skin rushed up to my nose. The sudden urge to suck his finger into the warm heat of my mouth made my taste buds water. Loud cracks of flesh on flesh reverberated through the door. I slammed my eyes shut. Oh, God, William was spanking Prue. She loved when William spanked her ass, and I enjoyed hearing how much she loved it. My nipples hardened under the flimsy material of my summer dress.

"Open your eyes, Kennedy," Marco whispered against the side of my face.

His warm breath brushed the shell of my ear, sending a ripple of goose bumps in unexpected awareness of him as a man. A hot, virile man. I squeezed my thighs together and shook my head. The sounds behind us grew even louder as Prue started begging. I wet my lips, licking Marco's finger with the movement.

He trailed his damp finger down from my lips to

my throat and pressed against the rapid pound of my pulse fluttering in my neck so hard even I could feel it.

"Open," he demanded in a heated whisper.

His tone whipped through my insides and sent a rush of arousal through my body, but I snapped open my eyes at his demand.

"Good girl," he praised in that same husky, demanding whisper tone.

A shiver of desire wracked my body. The sounds behind the door grew louder, more urgent. I shifted a fraction, and my stomach met the hardness of Marco's erection. A quiet whimper escaped my throat. My gaze stayed on the front of his pants, brushing against me with the tiniest of touches. The desire for what was inside filled me with urgency more than the air I breathed right now. I could take him in my hand or drop to my knees and take him in my mouth. All of it. I wanted to be screwed by him. Hard and furious up against this very door.

I sucked in a ragged breath, drawing his expensive aftershave deeper into my senses. I'd smelled him often enough over the years I'd worked for the Burberrys, but never this close, never this personal. We were mere acquaintances. I was the nanny. He was my boss's best friend. We had nothing in common. Never would. Except for this moment here, listening to Prue and William have sex.

I was burning up, my insides clenched with the need to experience the ecstasy, the pleasure, the release building in the air between us.

As if to stress my words, Prue screamed her orgasm through the solid door. Marco stepped back, dropping his hand from my neck. His gaze swept up and down me once, twice, as though he'd never seen me before in his life. A new awareness glittered in his eyes.

An understanding I was a dirty woman who enjoyed hearing other people have sex.

He smiled, a deep carnal smile promising many wicked delights, spun on his heel, strode to the front door, and let himself out. If I possessed the time, I'd sink to the floor, but I didn't. Prue and William had finished having sex and one or both would soon come through the door. I ran up the stairs and into my bedroom, my breath coming in short sharp rasps, not from the exertion but from what had happened between me and Marco.

Moments later, the unmistakable click of Prue's heels rose along the stairs and disappeared onto the thick plush carpeting in their bedroom. Every nerve ending sparked like I'd stuck my finger in an electric field. Perhaps I did. Marco's electric field. I stretched up on my tippy-toes to my secret hiding spot high on the bookshelf, my hand searching for the box of toys hidden amongst the books and bouquets of dried flowers. Taking the box down, I punched in the code and unlocked the lid. Out fell the dildo. I didn't even wait to get into bed. I yanked my panties aside, shoved the toy into my wetness hard and fast, imagining it was Marco's cock until I came against the bookshelf. My legs shaking and my eyes open as he'd told me to. Shame scorched a trail across my cheeks.

How would I ever look Marco in the eyes again now that he knew my secret?

## Chapter Two

*Now*

I'd successfully avoided Marco all month, apart from Prue's birthday pool party, which had been awkward as hell. Not an easy feat when he visited William at the mansion often. Aside from being his best friend, he was also his lawyer. The pair had been working hard the last month and now I knew why. William purchased a new business and named the venture after Prue for their wedding anniversary. Prue and William also renewed their wedding vows in the new endeavor at Prue's Paradise Resort and Day Spa.

The wedding I was a guest at.

William, dressed in a black tuxedo, spun Prue adorned in a long white gown around the dance floor once more. I hadn't seen them sneak off for a quickie during their wedding and to say they disappointed me was an understatement. They had a beautiful ceremony, though, and the reception was pretty. I tipped another glass of gin and tonic down my throat since the twins were staying at William's parents' tonight and I could party like the twenty-something woman I was. I could let my ponytail down from the confines of the hair tie, since there were no sticky fingers or paint the twins more often than not snuck into my hair.

A firm hand landed on my waist. The touch of Marco. He'd simply touched my chin and neck that night outside William's office, but I'd thought of him many nights since. The placement of his hand was possessive in a way that sent a thrill down my spine.

"Kennedy, your dress is exquisite," Marco said. "You are breathtaking."

I tilted my head. My long hair, which I always tied up in a ponytail at work, swished across my bare back. The plunging back of the aqua-green dress was from Tiffany, Prue's best friend, and a friend to me now. Tiffany was a fashion designer and since I didn't have the money for a gown to wear to the wedding, I couldn't very well turn down her offer of a gown. The way the silk fabric clung to every inch of my body left nothing to the imagination. I hadn't even been able to wear underwear because the lines showed under the fabric.

"Thank you," I forced out in politeness since the heat of his hand was playing havoc with my body.

"Care to dance?"

I jolted with surprise and swung his way. Big mistake. He was without doubt knee-quaking handsome in his black tuxedo and crisp white shirt. His gray eyes seemed darker than usual under his black eyelashes. His brown hair was slicked back, making me want to run my fingers through the strands and ruffle his composed exterior.

"No." I pursed my lips.

Hell no, if my body clamored for him now, what would it be like while we danced, our bodies moving together in rhythm?

"No?" He cocked an eyebrow.

"You heard me." I signaled the waiter for another drink.

Marco leaned closer, snaked his arm around my waist, and lowered his voice. "Let me put it this way. Dance with me."

His tone of voice sent a shiver of arousal racing through my body. I let him lead me onto the dance floor. *Fool.* But he knew my secret. He swept us into a dance, hips swaying in time to the others, and hands clasping each other's bodies. I tried not to think about those firm hands touching my body in other places. The places I'd imagined over the last month. I desperately tried not to think about the size of his erection last time we'd been this close. Or the sounds of sex we'd both listened to together.

The trouble was when you tried not to think of something, you always ended up thinking about it.

The song ended. I took a step back. He firmed his hold on me. Goose bumps erupted over my skin.

"Stay," he said, again in the tone that brooked no refusal and sent my body surging with need.

"Okay," I whispered.

"This dress is something else," he said, brushing his thumb over my bare lower back.

"Tiffany made it."

"It's like it's poured on you."

"I couldn't even wear underwear."

His thumb stopped for a second, then slid lower down my back and traced the edge of the dress.

"You shouldn't tell a man you're not wearing any underwear."

I tilted my chin up and at last stared him in the eyes. "Really? Why?" I fluttered my eyelashes, all innocent-like.

He let out a puff of a laugh. "We both know you're not innocent."

"I'm afraid I don't know what you're referring to."

His gray eyes darkened. "Kennedy," he rumbled. "You shouldn't tempt me."

"Tempt you to do what?"

He shook his head. "I don't do relationships."

"Everyone knows that." I dropped his gaze.

"Look at me," he commanded.

My gaze snapped to his once again. Damn, that tone got me every time. Raw hunger blazed back at me. I'd never had a man stare at me like he wanted to devour me before. It was liberating and unsettling.

I wet my lips. "I should go home."

His lips twitched.

"Alone."

"Very well, I'll drive you." He swung us to a stop and escorted me off the dance floor, all gentleman-like, so at odds with the expression he'd given me.

"No need, Gabe will drive me back to the mansion."

His brows puckered. "Gabe left hours ago."

"No way, I saw him at the bar before we started dancing."

"Which was hours ago." His lips quirked at the corners.

"Were we dancing that long?"

"Yes."

He placed his hand on my lower back once more and guided me through the beautifully decorated reception room and out of the resort. A crisp breeze blew in off the ocean, carrying the scent of salt water. I inhaled like I'd needed the next breath more than I did, trying to clear my senses of Marco. How did we dance for so long, and I hadn't even noticed?

The valet jumped into action and returned with Marco's sleek, red Chevrolet Camaro. I'd heard the rumble of the machine often enough over the years, but I'd never been inside the car or experienced a ride in it. A bit like the man. I smothered my giggle as I slid into his car. Marco drove like a race car driver, weaving through the heavy Los Angeles traffic and speeding through amber lights. I clutched the sides of the seat and prayed, even though I wasn't religious, we arrived at the mansion in one piece.

"Good grief," I snapped the moment the car stopped at the Burberry mansion. "Do you always drive like a maniac?"

He scowled. "There's nothing wrong with my driving."

"No?" I released my death grip on the car seat. "Do Prue and William let you drive the kids anywhere?"

"That's beside the point. I'm a great uncle."

"Ah-huh." I fumbled for the door handle.

His hand snapped across the car and grabbed mine. "Allow me."

"Fine." I pursed my lips.

Marco let go of my hand, climbed out of the driver's door, and rounded the car. I couldn't stop the way my eyes checked out his body while he wore a tuxedo. He was too sexy like this. Desire ran a raging river through my insides. What would it be like to have sex with a man like Marco? *Stop thinking about sex.* It will not happen. Prue and William wouldn't want us hooking up. It'd be too weird for their nanny to date their friend. Hired help and all.

He opened the car door. I swung my knees together to make sure I didn't flash him my lack of underwear and climbed out of the low-slung car.

"Thanks for the ride."

The corners of his lips twitched. Ride. I'd wanted to ride him ever since the night he'd caught me eavesdropping outside William's office. I couldn't stop thinking about it. About him.

"I'll … um … see you sometime?"

"Invite me in for coffee."

"That's not a good idea."

He let out a quiet breath. "You're right. Let me walk you to the door."

"Such a gentleman?"

"Is that a question?" His lips spread into a grin. "Or are you asking if I'd be ungentlemanly if you asked me in for coffee and I said yes?"

"Ha." I turned to the mansion.

His firm hand slid to my back. Damn it, I liked his touch. We walked up the stairs to the mansion, the sexual tension so thick I struggled to breathe through it.

I tapped the key code in for the door. Marco's fingers danced their way up my back and sunk into the thickness of my hair, sending a thousand sparks of pleasure shooting out from my scalp.

"The answer to your question is yes and no. When a woman permits me, I will treat her as ungentlemanly as she likes. Until then I'm always a gentleman."

I shoved open the door instead of asking him to treat me however he wanted. To defile me in any way. Every way.

"Good night, Kennedy," he said, his voice husky. Dark. Full of seduction and sex.

I stepped across the threshold and spun around. There was no way to hide the hard tips my nipples puckered into at his words.

"Good night, Marco."

He didn't so much as drop his gaze, but we were both aware of my body's response to him, his words, his nearness. Neither of us moved. Our chests synced their up and down movement as we breathed each other in.

The chime of his phone broke our staring contest. He swiped the cell out of his pants pocket.

Scowling at the screen, he muttered, "Archaic nonsense. What century do they think we're living in?"

"Is everything okay?"

"No." He tapped a response to whatever he'd received.

"Is there anything I can do to help? Even have the coffee you wanted?"

*I couldn't let him go, could I? No, I had to throw myself at him.*

He lifted his gaze from the cell and peered at me with wide eyes.

"Actually," he said, "there is something you can do. Have dinner with me tomorrow night."

He spoke in that commanding voice again and weak as will me, said, "Okay."

"I'll pick you up at seven."

He left me gaping after him. My pulse thudded under my skin in an infatuated and excited way. While my mouth fell open in a *holy shit, what have I done?*

## Chapter Three

*What had I gotten myself in for?* I glared at my reflection in the floor-length mirror. Once again, I'd left my hair down and put on a sexy dress, except for this dress I could wear a thong underneath. A small piece of armor against whatever would happen tonight. Did I want Marco to be ungentlemanly with me? Yes, yes, I did. Would I tell him? No.

I was a chicken. I may as well cluck like one, too.

The loud rumbling engine of his Camaro sounded as he drove up to the front of the mansion. I'd never pictured myself living in a mansion since I was from a small country town. This rich life was never on my horizon until my ex-boyfriend dumped me as fast as he could when I'd lost our baby because of an ectopic pregnancy. Then the other blow arrived with the news from the doctors. The scarring in my fallopian tube complicated my chance of having further children and the likelihood of it happening again was high.

Everywhere I'd turned in Lake Havasu City reminded me of my time with my childhood sweetheart, from the walking trails to the water sports, and the café where he'd buy me my favorite milkshake, and the places we'd made love. I'd been so sure we were in love. But how could we be when he'd left me while still in the hospital recovering from surgery? Who did that?

I'd left Arizona and traveled to California, hoping the sunshine and beaches would bring joy back into my life. Prue found me in the park across the street from William's office one day when I'd been wandering without direction, searching for something, anything to make the heartache go away. I was at my lowest low, seeing the kids playing in the playground and knowing I'd never have them myself.

To say the incident made me jaded, bitter, and an emotional mess was an understatement. Prue sat next to me on the bench in the park, handed me a tissue, and told me she'd had sex with her husband hoping it would bring on labor. I'd taken one glance at her gorgeous, flushed face and understood why he'd want to. She'd then rubbed her very pregnant stomach. My gaze glued to her pregnancy bump like she might give birth any second. Envy clawed at my eyelids and my tears dried. I'd blurted out how I'd lost my baby to this stranger, and how my ex-boyfriend left me. So unlike me. But Prue was amazing. She'd wrapped her arm around my shoulder, told me she didn't have a clue what she was doing and needed a nanny who'd love her kids as much as her.

And so, my life now possessed a purpose. I loved her twins. They'd never be mine. I understood that, but I loved them just the same.

The doorbell chimed, transporting me back to the here and now. I took one last glimpse at myself and my flat stomach that would never hold a baby. The reason I'd never dated since coming here. How did you start a relationship with a man and then reveal you can't have children unless they're willing to help you undergo fertility treatment?

Too complicated.

It was easier to stay single, get orgasms from my toys, and watch other people have sex. There was nothing wrong with what I did.

The doorbell chimed again. *How long had I been standing here?*

I hurried down the stairs, careful not to twist my ankle in the heels. Heels weren't part of the nanny wardrobe. I couldn't chase twin boys in heels, but I enjoyed wearing them. Not that I ever went out anywhere to wear them. The image of Prue in her underwear and heels flashed into my mind. Would I dress up in sexy lingerie like her if I had a husband? Would I wear lingerie and heels for Marco?

I yanked open the front door. My heart skittered to a stop. Marco looked good enough to strip in a deep-gray suit and tie, exuding wealth and power like the way an onion reeked.

"Hi." I ran my fingers through my hair.

"Kennedy." He smiled. "You look different with your hair down. I forgot to say that yesterday at the wedding."

"Same me." I shut the door and keyed in the password.

"No," he said, placing his firm hand on my back. "You appear like a teenager when you have your hair in a ponytail and wear your cute little dresses or shorts. Now, you seem like a sinful woman."

"Sinful, hey?" I stopped at his car. "No one has ever called me that before."

He dropped his hand from my back and opened the door. I climbed into the Camaro.

Marco leaned through the door. "Depends on your definition of sin."

I scanned his face, from the top of his head and the thickness of his brown hair to the mischief in his gray eyes, the proud tip of his nose, and the fullness of his lips. That face. His lips were made for sin. He could have been carved from the Devil himself. He shut the door and slid into the driver's seat, all confidence, and man. Thick thighs strained against his suit pants, and his suit jacket tugged across his chest.

"There are seven sins, to be precise. Pride, greed, lust, envy, gluttony, wrath, and sloth." He ran his heated gaze over my body. "And you, sweet woman, possess all of them."

"Explain," I huffed, crossing my arms over my chest, then flung them to the sides of the car seat as he sped off.

"You have oodles of pride."

"I do not."

His eyebrow rose a fraction. "You're greedy for what William and Prue have."

I snapped my mouth shut. So what if I wanted a passionate relationship like theirs? Who wouldn't?

"You lust after both of them."

I narrowed my eyes on the profile of his face and said, "I don't."

"No?" He tilted his head to the side. "Then what do you call it when you listen to them have sex?"

"I…" I swung my gaze out the window. "It's not what you think."

"That's what everyone says." He shifted the gears and sped around a corner. "Then there's the envy of you wanting to be bent over and taken hard from behind."

Oh, dear Lord. I sucked in a breath, inhaling his expensive aftershave in a gush of wanton desire. I wanted him to take me in any way more than anything.

"Kennedy, Kennedy," he tsked and clucked his tongue. "I've seen you eat copious amounts of cake in a gluttonous way. Yet, you're as tiny as a dancer."

"So what if I like cake?" I spun in the seat to face him. "You haven't seen me angry?"

He stopped at a red light and swung his gaze to my face. "Haven't I?"

"Shut up." I ground my teeth.

The traffic light flashed green, and he floored the car so fast my head flung back into the seat.

"Then there's sloth. The sin that drags you down the most. You keep yourself looking like a teenager instead of embracing your womanhood. If that's not sloth, then I don't know what is."

I clenched my fingers on the car seat harder, digging my nails into the leather, hoping they'd leave marks. Serve him right, the arrogant bastard.

"What about you?" I snapped. "As if you don't have any of those traits."

"I do," he agreed with ease.

He turned into the valet parking area of the impressive Beverly Intercontinental. The building seemed like a castle out of a fairy tale with its flags flying in the circular driveway.

"I don't fool myself that I don't have them."

The valet attendant opened the door. I climbed out before Marco could stop me. Back straight, I marched to the entrance. Marco stalked over to me, his face drawn tight in disapproval.

"Don't be a brat," he whispered in that demanding tone.

"Excuse me?" I cocked a hip, trying to not let his tone get to me again and holding onto the raging emotions he'd sparked to life by a few words. "You said some not very nice things about me and I'm being a brat? Well, too bad if I'm not happy. I'm leaving."

"No, you're not." He clasped my elbow in a grip that was firm but not hard. "You're going to put a smile on your pretty face and walk into the restaurant with me and we're going to have a pleasant dinner."

"And to think," I hissed, "I thought about having sex with you last night."

He chuckled. "You've thought about having sex with me many nights."

"I have not," I spluttered.

"Adding liar to the list, are we?"

I jabbed my elbow into his ribs. He grunted. A

surge of satisfaction ran through my veins.

"Oh, sweetheart." He gripped my elbow a fraction harder and ran his thumb over the sensitive skin of my inner arm. "So much sexual tension. When was the last time you've been truly fucked?"

His husky question sent a shiver down my back picturing him being the one to truly fuck me.

"None of your business," I snapped, then shut my mouth as we walked by the wealthy patrons inside the hotel. More than one snooty woman peered down their noses at me. Pasting a smile on my face, I lifted my chin and sashayed inside the restaurant. Marco's fingers branded my arm in his commanding grip with each step, but I wouldn't fight his hold in front of this many people and cause a scene. Besides, my skin was alive with electricity beneath his fingers.

"Good evening, Mr. Lawrence, your table is ready in the private room. This way please." The maître d' greeted and escorted us through the restaurant to a row of doors on the side of the main eating area. He held one door open and we shuffled inside, me too reluctant to be alone with Marco now he'd shown his arrogant side, and Marco too reluctant to let go of my elbow like he sensed I'd turn and walk out of the restaurant.

The maître d' gave us an indulgent smile and drew out my chair. Marco let go of my arm and I settled in the plush red velvet seat like I was royalty. The maître d' flicked the bright white napkin over my lap, then Marco's, then he left the opulent room. I took in the fancy crystal wineglasses, the swirling blue pattern on the plates, and the cutlery polished to within an inch of being blinding bright. A posy of roses and hydrangeas sat between us. I glared at Marco over them.

"Why are you being an asshole?" I asked.

He shrugged his shoulders. I couldn't stop myself

from admiring the way the suit rippled. Even being an ass, he was attractive.

"It's better you know who I am before you have delusions of me being a nice guy and planning to live happily ever after with me."

"Are you freaking kidding me? Who said anything about happily ever after?"

The door swung open, and a waiter walked in, placed entrée dishes on the table, and backed out without a word.

"What's this?" I lifted my shiny fork and stabbed at the food on the plate.

"Sauteed sea scallops with caramelized apples and chicken livers."

"Chicken livers?" I shook my head. "Rich people are crazy."

"Eat them, you'll like them."

"We'll see." I speared a bit of everything onto my fork and shoved the food in my mouth, hoping mixing it altogether would stop me from thinking about the fact I had chicken livers in my mouth. I swallowed. "Not the worst thing I've put in my mouth."

"And what was the worst thing?"

"Hmm." I ate another forkful. "My ex-boyfriend's dick. He had weird tasting jizz."

Marco gagged on his food. I smirked. Score one for me. He sipped from the water glass, his pink tongue flicking out to coat his lips in a glisten of moisture, making them appear kissable and oh-so-alluring.

"Does this ex-boyfriend have a name?"

"Julius." I dragged my gaze from his lips. "Not that it matters. He's back in Lake Havasu City, married with three kids."

"You're from Arizona?"

"Yes." I placed my fork on the plate of the almost

eaten entrée.

I watched him finish his dish and the way the fork slid into his lips. The slight peak of his tongue with each mouthful and the way his jaw clenched and unclenched as he chewed. And then the way his throat swallowed. Seemed I couldn't keep my eyes off his mouth for too long.

"What's this dinner about, Marco? This isn't a date with the way you insulted me right now to prove you're a dick."

"No, it's not a date." He placed his fork on the plate with a soft clink and picked up the wine bottle from the ice bucket. "Wine?"

"No." I placed my hand over the top of the wineglass, sensing I'd need my wits about me for this conversation.

He put the wine bottle back without filling his glass. "As you know, I'm a lawyer."

"Mm-hmm. No big news there."

"My firm wants to make me a senior partner and the face of their business." He ran a hand over his tie. "They say I've got the face for it."

I ran my eyes over his handsome face again. No hardship there.

"I can see that."

The waiter walked into the private room interrupting us and collected our plates. Silence descended in the room. The place was cozy, and in any other circumstances, I would have found the atmosphere romantic. How many women had Marco brought here for a romantic dinner? Plenty, by the way the maître d' greeted him. I crossed my legs under the table and placed my fists in my lap. Why did the thought of Marco with other women make me angry? Everyone knew he wasn't into relationships. William and Prue joked about his string of dates often enough for me to get the picture of his life. When the waiter left, he cleared his throat.

"They'd prefer me to have the family image too."

"Sorry, I'm not following."

"I need a wife."

## Chapter Four

"What does needing a wife have to do with our dinner … oh." I snapped my mouth shut.

The waiter appeared with our meals, deposited them on the table without a single word, then backed out of the room with a tight smile and a small bow. Poor guy. I'd leave him a tip for his discreet service.

"What's this now?" I lifted my fork.

"Creamy spinach-stuffed salmon."

"You like seafood?"

"I do." He scooped food into his mouth.

I sat transfixed for a solid minute. A wife. Did he mean me? Of course he didn't. I put my fork down unable to eat without knowing what this was.

"Marco, what? I mean… What?"

He laughed. The sound was deep and so full of amusement that my lips twitched. A sound I'd heard many times when he'd spent time at the Burberry mansion. Often it involved the twins making him laugh. Me making him laugh sent a tiny thrill through my body even if it was because he'd confused me.

"As I said, I need a wife, I don't do relationships, but I need one on paper, and someone to go to business dinner meetings, that sort of thing, be pleasant and talk to the other wives. A woman with the wholesome girl-next-door appearance, which I thought was you, but the last two nights you've looked like a sex siren."

"What would I get out of it?" I asked, brushing aside his sex siren comment.

"That's what tonight is for. We negotiate the terms."

"Negotiate marriage?" I picked up my fork. "You're crazy."

"Logical."

He ate his meal, and I ate mine.

The fish was excellent, but I'd expected as much when we'd arrived at the hotel. The first and only time I was here was when Prue needed someone to fill a seat for a charity event. She'd loaned me a dress for the ball, and that night Tiffany signed a business contract with her two boyfriends, a type of marriage in the only way three people could get married. All thanks to Marco too.

The man had an eye for contracts, that was for sure.

What could I ask for in a marriage? Anything. He was wealthy, his family came from a small fortune, and he earned a lot as a lawyer working for the rich and famous in Los Angeles. There wasn't anything I could ask for that he couldn't give except for love and a baby. Those things weren't an option for me anyway.

"So shall we start the negotiations?"

"Wait a minute," I said. "How and when would we get married?"

"I can draw up the contract tonight. We can sign the prenuptial agreement tomorrow and head straight for the county recorder's office."

"I have the twins during the day." I pointed out the flaw in his crazy plan.

"William's parents would keep them for the day too if you asked."

"No." I scowled. "They're my duty during the day while Prue and William are on their honeymoon."

"I guess we could wait until they get back."

My scowl deepened.

The waiter returned and cleared our plates.

"If I'm considering this, negotiation one…" I placed my hands on the table. I wasn't considering this anyway but just so he knew a wedding at the county recorder's office wouldn't fly. A quick ceremony wouldn't be appropriate with whoever else he picked. I may as well do the woman a favor. "There will be no wedding at the county recorder's office. It'll be a proper wedding with family and friends present."

"I need this to happen sooner rather than later, and wedding planning takes months, sometimes years."

"I could plan a wedding in one month."

His eyebrows shot into his hair.

The waiter returned with dessert. An entire cake. Not a cake you'd pick up at a store, but one covered in a rich chocolate glaze, white chocolate curls on top, and around the edge a rim of gold-flecked flowers. He set the cake down and placed the dessert plates on the table, then the waiter cut the cake and served it. If I didn't love cake so much it might upset me that he cut the masterpiece.

"Thank you," I said.

The waiter flashed me a smile then backed up out of the door.

"Are you trying to fatten me up or sweeten me up?" I dug my fork into the cake and rolled my eyes back in bliss as the decadent chocolate melted on my tongue.

"Neither. I know you like cake."

"Hmm…" I hummed around another mouthful of cake.

"You can organize a wedding in a month?"

I swallowed the cake. "If I said yes, and I'm not saying I am, my family will want to come, and they won't believe I'd get married at an office. And then there's Prue and William, they'd want to be there."

"It's not a genuine marriage."

"So, you want me to sign my life over to you for nothing?"

"Not nothing. You'd have money, a home, financial security, you could work any job you want."

"I'm working the job I want already."

"You want to be a nanny?"

"I do and I love it."

"That might be a problem then." He tugged on his tie again.

"Yes, you didn't think about my job, did you?" I cocked an eyebrow. "Prue's having another baby soon and she'll need me."

"As if I could forget she's pregnant."

"What's that supposed to mean?"

"Nothing," he mumbled.

"See, right away this won't work. You'll need to find another wife."

Marco sighed and leaned back in his chair. "No, it has to be you. You're perfect for the role."

"It can't be me." I cut another slice of cake and put it on my plate.

He snapped forward and grabbed my wrist holding the knife. "It's you, or I tell William and Prue you listen to them have sex, probably even watch them too."

I gasped. "You wouldn't."

"Watch me. Then we'll see if they want you to still be their nanny. You'll never see those kids again and you won't have anything to do with the baby."

My heart raced, as fear and panic flared to life. To lose my job, the kids I loved, the friend I'd made in Prue. The back of my throat burned.

"Screw you." I twisted my hand.

He held tight, his fingers an iron band around the thudding of my pulse. "That's what you want, isn't it? I'm open to adding sex to the marriage."

"You're a real piece of work."

"Thank you." He smiled like I'd complimented him and let go of my wrist. "Besides, we'll have to consummate the marriage at least once for it to be legal."

31

I puffed out a breath, then shoveled the cake into my mouth like my favorite food would solve this problem. Maybe by the time I finished the second piece, I'd have found a way out of this. But with each delicious mouthful of chocolate cake, my hopes vanished.

"You're blackmailing me into marrying you?"

"I prefer to call it negotiating."

"Call it what you want, we both know what this is."

He shrugged. I bet he was a shark in his job. I could picture him like those lawyers in the movies getting everything they want.

"So far, we have negotiated a proper wedding in a month, and sex, anything else?"

"If, and I'm still saying a big if here, I agree to this, then you can't screw other women."

"I wouldn't, it'd hurt the family image the firm wants. The same goes for you."

"I don't ... I mean ... I wouldn't."

He studied me with his intense deep gray eyes. "When *was* the last time you had sex?"

I flattened my lips together.

"That long?" His lips twitched.

"If you mean sex with other people, then it's been a while, if you mean sex with me then it was ten minutes before you picked me up."

He chuckled. "Oh, Kennedy, I never realized you had this super sexed-up version hiding under the teen appearance. Well, not until I caught you eavesdropping on William and Prue, that is." He stretched across the table and lightly traced his finger up the inside of my wrist over the place he'd gripped. "You keep her wrapped up pretty tight, don't you? Hiding under the image of the sweet country girl and perfect nanny."

A thousand sparks of pleasure burst free from his

simple touch. My skin ignited like it was on fire.

"Do you listen to them often?" he asked, his voice dropping to a huskier tone.

"Yes," I murmured then cleared my voice and said, "It's hard not to when their bedroom is near mine."

"Watch them too?"

I dropped my chin to my chest and stared at the remaining cake. Could I eat a third piece? At least if I was eating, I wouldn't have to talk. He tipped my chin up with his firm finger.

"Do you?" he asked in a demanding tone.

A shiver of desire ran down my spine. "Yes."

"Good girl," he husked out. "There's no shame in enjoying watching sex. I find it quite erotic myself."

"You do?" My pulse jumped as his finger drifted higher up my arm to the crease of my elbow, the one he'd manhandled earlier, but I didn't care about that. All I cared about was how far he'd trace his finger over my aching skin.

"I even video myself if a woman is agreeable and signs a contract giving me permission, along with a nondisclosure agreement."

My jaw dropped open. His finger met the bare skin of my upper arm, and higher across my shoulder. Goose bumps exploded over my skin. Higher still his finger trailed across my collarbone, the length of my neck, then he tapped my chin shut.

"When we're married, we can watch them together if you like?"

I nodded my head. Eager to see this man in a sex video. I tucked my foot behind my leg and squeezed my thighs together, aroused by the idea in a way that everything ached.

"Are you wearing underwear tonight?"

"Yes."

"Shame," he said. "I could have slipped my hand under the table right here in this private room, and under the sexy dress you're wearing."

My eyelids fluttered closed in a slow blink imagining the soft stroke of his hand up my thigh the way he'd traced it up to my arm.

"The question is," he said, tangling his fingers in my hair. "Would I find you wet?"

I licked my lips. "I guess you won't find out."

His fingers combed through my hair sending tingles racing through my scalp and down my body centering in the one place I longed for Marco to touch me most. The place he would indeed find me wet.

"Perhaps not tonight." He let go of my hair and sat back in his seat. "What else should we negotiate?"

"You, ah…" I scrambled to get my mind back on track. One brief touch from him and I was ready to explode. "You said you wanted a family image, does that mean you want children too?"

"No," he snapped, his body stiffening.

The entire atmosphere changed in the room.

"Why not? You're not getting any younger."

"Is that your way of saying I'm too old for you?"

"I'm twenty-nine and you're forty-three, I don't think you're too old for me."

"Good." He nodded. "You may as well know I can't have kids, not without a lot of hassle."

"I'm sorry," I said, my voice catching at the end with the emotion burning in my throat. I understood his pain too well.

"Nothing for you to be sorry for. It happened a long time ago in college. William got in a bar fight, the man pulled a gun, I tackled him to the ground and suffered a blow to my balls in the process. I didn't think the injury was as bad as it was. Those damn things hurt when they take a beating."

I sucked in a harsh breath. "Sounds painful."

"It was. All good now, but my swimmers aren't the best for getting the job done in normal circumstances."

"I'm not sure I want kids anyway," I murmured. My medical issues would make it hard and with Marco's issues, then it might be impossible for us to have children. Besides, people shouldn't bring kids into the world unless they'd love them unconditionally. Marco loved William and Prue's kids but that didn't mean he'd love his own.

It was stupid to think, but he'd shown me the asshole side of him tonight and I wasn't sure I liked that part of him.

Or whether it turned me on more than the other side of him.

Shit, this negotiation was going downhill fast.

I squared my shoulders. "I want to still be Prue's nanny."

"All right, but just during the day. I'll need you at night."

He'd need me at night for what? Dinner business meetings like when Prue accompanied William. Or sex? Or both?

"If you can get Prue to agree to that, then okay, I guess we sort of have a deal."

"Prue doesn't own you. We have a deal."

## Chapter Five

I stared at the chocolate cake like it was the evidence last night had happened. Dinner ended straight after he'd uttered the words, "We have a deal." The waiter boxed up the leftover cake and I'd hugged it to my chest and carried the box to Marco's car like a prize. He'd dropped me back at the Burberry mansion, walked me to the door like a gentleman, and told me he'd be by tomorrow night with the prenuptial agreement for me to read over and make any changes.

I cut another piece of cake and ate it with my fingers. So what if I'd eaten a slice for breakfast this morning? I deserved cake what with this crazy marriage proposal, if I could even call it that. And so what if I was eating another slice for dinner? I'd taken the twins to the zoo hoping to wear them out for William's parents and a goat in the petting zoo turned into a vicious ninja and kicked me in the thigh. I'd walked around the zoo with a dead leg and no doubt a blossoming bruise. The boys thought it funny. I hadn't.

The doorbell chimed signaling my soon-to-be husband had arrived at the Burberry mansion.

What a joke.

Licking my fingers, I walked from the kitchen to the front door.

I flung open the door as though I was about to face down my worst nightmare and snapped, "Come in."

"Is that any way to greet your fiancé?" Marco stepped forward, crowding my space, and shut the door behind his back.

I didn't budge even though it meant the material of our clothes brushed and rippled against my body. "Pretty sure we're not engaged."

He raised an eyebrow. "I beg to differ."

"Wrong." I shifted away from him. His damn aftershave was getting to me again. "Engaged people have a ring." I waved my left hand in front of his face.

He slid his hand into the top of his suit jacket and withdrew a blue velvet box. "Like this?" He popped the lid.

Holy cow. The diamond was huge. The ring sparkled as if the diamond exhibited an internal light. I gulped. This was happening.

Marco picked up my left hand, took the ring from the box, and slid the massive diamond onto my finger. The platinum-gold band fit like he'd had the ring made for me. I should have guessed it would. Marco turned my hand under the light and all I could stare at was the huge-ass diamond.

"What have you got on your fingers?"

"Oh, cake." I giggled.

He shook his head, raised my hand to his lips, and sucked a finger into his mouth. His tongue swirled around the tip of my finger then ran the length of it. He shifted onto the next finger, licking and cleaning my skin in the same way he did the first. I wanted to slam my eyes shut but the way my finger disappeared into his mouth glued my gaze to the motion. He turned me on with each swirl of his tongue around the tip before dipping lower. My clit ached imagining his tongue circling the hard bud in the same way. By the time he finished all my fingers, I was almost ready to throw him to the floor or the door. He moved onto my thumb. A tiny whimper escaped my mouth.

Marco met my gaze. His eyes blazed passionate and heady. I dropped the intense stare and peered straight through his suit and pictured him naked as though I was a superhero. Over the years, I'd seen the man enough times in the Burberry pool in his board shorts, to know every dip and hollow in his firm chest and the enticing V disappearing into his shorts. I wasn't a superhero, simply a woman with a splendid memory.

"There you go, all clean now." He let go of my hand.

Yet I was a dirty, dirty woman.

I cleared my throat. "Did you bring the papers?"

"Why, Kennedy, are you eager to sign them now?"

I crossed my arms over my chest to hide my hard nipples. The man turned me into a big bundle of raging need from licking my fingers. How was it even possible? Fingers weren't an erogenous zone, were they?

"I want to get it over and done with."

"Such sweet words from my fiancé." He chuckled. "Let's do this in William's office, shall we?"

"I ... ah ... I don't go in there."

"No?" He cocked his head. "I do, it's where we discuss business. Seems like the right place to do it, don't you think?"

Do it? Did he mean sex? *Get your mind off sex.* This was blackmail. I squared my shoulders.

"After you." He waved his hand.

Head high, I walked down the hallway. His heavy footsteps followed my quieter ones since I was barefoot, while he wore a gorgeous navy-blue suit, pale-blue tie, white shirt, and shiny black dress shoes.

"Ladies always come first," he husked out in that tone of his that sent my insides clenching with need.

I half-turned, about to give him a retort, but I stepped wrong. Shooting pain flared in my thigh. I stumbled a step. His firm hands were on my waist in an instant keeping me upright.

"Ow." Tears welled in my eyes.

"Did you twist your ankle?" His gaze dropped to

my feet.

"No, I'm okay. You can let go now." My damn body was on fire with his hands holding me.

"Kennedy, don't lie to me. I don't like it and I won't have us lying to each other. We need to be honest or we will end up hating each other."

"Who says I don't already hate you?" I bit my lip.

He raised his eyes to my face, his lips firming into a tight line. "I lived with a liar once, I won't do it again."

My heart exploded with sympathy for Marco. Stupid heart. But I knew about being lied to. Lies you were the one. Lies they loved you. That you'd have a family together. Live happily ever after. All lies. I hated them too. I didn't hate Marco though. He'd pissed me off with his tactics, but I was too damn attracted to him to hate him.

"I don't hate you," I whispered.

"I know you don't," he said lowering his voice. "If you did, I wouldn't have asked you to do this. I never wanted to say what I did, but you forced my hand."

I sighed. "A goat kicked me in the leg at the zoo today."

His tight lips eased apart and kicked up into a smile.

"Don't you dare laugh."

"I'm not." He held up his hands. "Let me see."

"Fine."

He picked me up and placed me on the shiny glass hallway table.

"Here?" I squeaked.

"There's no one else home."

I eased the edge of my denim skirt up along my legs—by chance it wasn't one of my skintight skirts, but the material was tight enough that I struggled to get it high enough while sitting. Marco's amused smile teased the edges of his lips, but he said nothing until I revealed the hoof-shaped bruise.

"I hope you killed the goat," he said, a deep scowl tugging his brows.

I laughed. "No, and I would have made the twins and the entire zoo full of children cry if I did."

He picked me up in his arms.

"What are you doing?" I screeched, wrapping my legs around his waist and clinging to him like a monkey.

"You should rest and put ice on the bruise." He carried me into William's office and placed me in a chair. "Stay there."

He disappeared and returned moments later with an ice pack. With care, he laid the ice over the bruise.

"Thanks," I said because it was the right thing to say. This side of Marco made up for his asshole attitude yesterday. This was the Marco I was used to seeing. Also, the one I hadn't thought about in a romantic or relationship sort of way in the three years we'd known each other. *What was up with that?* Sure, I'd noticed he was handsome, but that was as far as my thoughts traveled regarding Marco. Was it the asshole who attracted me? If so, how messed up was I?

Marco sat in the chair next to me, withdrew an envelope from his breast pocket, and handed it to me. I slid the papers out and flicked them open.

My name and Marco's were in bold writing across the top of the many pages underneath.

"How big is this thing?"

"You'll find out on our wedding night."

I rolled my eyes. "I'm not talking about your dick."

As if I hadn't seen the size of him in his wet board shorts anyway. The man was hung. A tiny flutter flickered between my legs and buried itself deep inside me, begging to take what he was offering. I lifted the ice pack. His warm hand landed over mine.

"Keep it there for twenty minutes."

"But it's cold." I pouted.

"Poor baby," he crooned. "Want me to kiss it better?"

All I pictured was the thickness of his hair between my legs kissing me better, but not the bruise, the place between my legs throbbing with need.

"Hmm, perhaps you do?" He dropped to his knees, lifted the ice pack, and kissed the bruise, his lips soft, gentle even.

"I ... um..."

"Yes?" He peered up at me and it was sexy as hell having him on his knees in front of me.

"Thanks," I said again. "That worked, it's like you've got magic lips." I couldn't help the sarcasm since he was pushing all the wrong buttons. Right buttons? I needed to remember this was blackmail. Not love or lust or even anything within the area of a normal relationship.

He smirked but said nothing.

I flicked the papers again and turned my attention from the hot sight of him inches from my aching core. My mind kept flickering back to the way he'd licked my fingers. I couldn't read a damn word.

"Can you sit in the chair?" I snapped.

He snorted. "I never knew you had this much attitude."

"Me?" I lowered the papers to my lap hoping he wouldn't catch the scent of my desire, because I was sure I could smell it. "What about you? You've been Mr. Nice Guy the entire time I've known you and now this." I waved the papers in the air.

"I am a lawyer." He sat back in the chair.

I needed him in the chair, but the dirty woman inside of me wanted him back between my legs doing more than kissing a bruise.

"All right, let's get this over with and you can leave." I smoothed the papers on the desk.

"Eager to get rid of me?"

"If I'm going to be stuck with you for life, then I plan to enjoy my alone time now."

"For Christ's sake, Kennedy, why do you have to be difficult?"

"Me?" I asked again.

"Yes, you. I won't expect a lot from you in this marriage. It'll be as convenient as I can make it, for you and me. It would be nice if we could at least get along like we used to."

I slumped back in the seat. He was right, we were on pleasant terms and now we'd gone to enemies. Could we go back to being friendly acquaintances?

"If you weren't blackmailing me, things might be different."

He dropped back to his knees. "You're right, that was assholish of me. I should have asked you as a friend if you would please help me out." He placed his hands on my knees and peered up at me with his deep-gray eyes.

My heart somersaulted inside my chest along with a fresh surge of desire.

"Why me?" I whispered.

"Because we always got along amicably, up until now that is, and you don't eyeball me like I'm a walking dollar sign like other women. They pretend to love me when they don't. I don't need to worry about love with you. I think we could have a convenient marriage." He rubbed his lips together. "I'm too used to saying whatever I need to get the job done. I won't tell William and Prue about your penchant for watching them have sex."

My lips twitched up into a small smile. His words eased the anger bubbling inside me since he'd threatened to take away all I cared for. But maybe this could work too. If I married Marco, then I'd always be in the Burberry's life. I'd see the children grow after they no longer needed a nanny. "Okay."

"Yes?"

"Yes." I shoved my left hand in his face. "You gave me this rock and I'm not giving the ring back. You're stuck with me now."

He laughed, sending his warm breath gusting over my bare thighs and higher under my skirt. My thigh muscles tensed. Marco's gaze dropped to my legs like he'd noticed the slight twitch of my muscles. He inhaled slow and deep like he was desperate for oxygen while my breathing stopped altogether.

"Spread your legs," he commanded in that tone that sent shivers dancing down my spine.

I shook my head. He'd see how damp my panties were if I obeyed him.

"Good girls get rewarded," he said in a way that sounded like a purr.

I gulped in a breath and oxygen rushed into my lungs making my head swim with the blast. Could I be a good girl? With Marco on his knees before me, I longed to do what he said.

"What sort of reward?"

His grin turned carnal, and his eyebrow rose to let me know it was indeed what I was imagining.

"You'll find out. Or you won't."

I eased my legs apart until cool air met my warm dampness.

"Pretty pink panties," he said. "I bet you're as pink underneath them." His thumbs urged my knees apart.

My skirt slid higher up my legs until the material bunched around my waist. My entire panties were now on display and the heated expression on Marco's face said he liked them. Liked them a lot. He inched forward and placed his mouth over my damp crotch, and with one solid suck my back bowed off the chair.

"Oh. That sort of reward." I ground against his face eager to end the incessant throbbing in my clit.

He rubbed his teeth over my clit, then lifted his head. "Are you a dirty girl, Kennedy?"

I shoved my hands in his hair and tried to tug his face back to my aching core, but he wrenched my fingers free taking a few strands of hair with us and slammed our hands on the arms of the chair holding me still.

"I asked you a question. I didn't say you could touch me."

My eyes narrowed to slits. "I didn't say you could touch me either."

"You want your reward, don't you?"

If that meant he'd place his mouth back on me, then yes, I did.

"Yes." I licked my lips. "I'm a dirty girl."

His lips spread into a seductive grin. "Do I need your permission to give you an orgasm?"

"No," I whispered. But I'd give it to him if that's what it would take for Marco to put his mouth back between my legs.

As if my no was all the permission he needed, he placed his mouth back on my damp panties. His tongue speared into the fabric shoving it deeper inside me while his teeth scraped over the satin covering my clit. I rocked my hips against his face chasing the building orgasm since he still had my hands clamped to the arms of the chair. He hadn't even touched my skin with his bare tongue, and I was so worked up that … oh … yes … my release was quick and hard against his face. My fingers clenched and unclenched on the arms of the chair as I rode out the orgasm until the last quiver subsided.

Marco released my hands and rocked back on his heels, a self-satisfied smirk stretching those lips which transported me to the best orgasm I'd enjoyed in a long while.

"Shut up," I said, tugging my skirt back down my legs.

"No need to be ashamed, sweetheart." He picked up the forgotten ice pack and placed it back on my leg, then sat back in his chair. "We all have needs." He tapped the papers. "I think you'll find this will cater to all of yours."

I picked up the papers, shocked to find my hands trembling. It was the orgasm, nothing else. Not the way Marco accepted my dirty side. Nope, not that at all. I read through the contract while Marco watched my every facial expression. It was unnerving being with someone who seemed to get me so well even though we hadn't spent time alone getting to know each other. I guess three years as acquaintances had rubbed off on us and we'd picked up things about each other we hadn't even realized.

Like he knew how much I loved eating cake.

How much I loved the twins.

Now he knew how much I loved getting off. I was pretty sure I'd screamed out a few things while he'd buried his face between my legs. The worst part was, I didn't even get to experience his tongue on me. In me. A shiver danced down my spine.

"Are you getting cold?" He slid the ice pack off my thigh and inspected the bruise.

"No." I picked up a pen and changed the subject

before I asked him to go down on me again. "Okay, I want you to change a few things."

"Such as?"

"This baby clause saying there are to be no children. While I don't think I want kids now, I don't want the choice taken away from me."

He crossed his arms. "Children would require IVF."

"I'm aware of the situation, and you may as well know I have issues in the reproductive department too. IVF is the only way for me too."

"I see." He uncrossed his arms. "In that case, how about we change the clause so there's a time limit? I mean, you're almost thirty."

"Twenty-nine."

"Let's say if we haven't changed our minds before you're forty then it's a no-go forever, and it has to be a joint decision to have them."

"I'm pretty sure I couldn't do IVF without you. I'd need your sperm to make it work."

"You would." He took the pen from my hand and scribbled the amendments across the papers. "Anything else?"

"Yes, I want to live near here."

"A house?"

"I don't see any apartments on this street, do you?"

He stared at me for a solid minute. "I have a pleasant apartment."

"I'm sure you have a nice bachelor pad somewhere in the city, but I want to be near the kids in case I'm needed, I can come over straightaway. It'll be bad enough when I tell Prue I'm getting married."

"She'll get over it. She couldn't expect someone as beautiful as you to never get married."

"Did you call me beautiful?" I placed my hands in my lap and twisted my fingers together.

"I've always thought you were beautiful," he said in his husky tone. "Even more now your face and chest are flushed a delicate pink from an orgasm."

"Thank you," I said. I was thanking him a lot tonight, and I enjoyed doing it. I enjoyed seeing the smile my thanks brought to his face, and the way his gray eyes sparkled with happiness like no one ever thanked him. "That's all I want to change."

"So, no objections to sex then?" He folded the papers and shoved them back into the envelope.

"You're asking me that after you put your mouth on me?"

"Well, yes." He shrugged in an adorable boyish way.

I laughed. "I have no objections to sex in our marriage."

"Ah," he said. "You want to wait until we're married?"

"You're the one who talked about consummating the marriage on our wedding night."

"That was before I found out how easy you come." He tucked the envelope into his suit and stood. "I guess this is going to be a long month for both of us."

"I've gone way longer than a month, it'll be easy."

He snorted, leaned over me, and brushed a kiss on the side of my cheek. "You'll ask me for sex before the month is over."

I shoved at his chest. "Other way around, mister."

"We'll see." He straightened. "Don't get up, I'll see myself out."

As he walked out of the office door, I watched the way his slacks brushed over his ass and knew he was right. I'd most likely ask him for sex before the end of the week let alone the month.

## Chapter Six

My phone blared with my annoying ringtone before the alarm. No one ever called me this early. I scrambled for the cell and swiped to answer without checking the caller ID, thinking it was an emergency with the twins.

"Hello?"

"Good morning, fiancée."

Marco's husky voice drifted down the line.

"What time is it?"

"Five thirty," he said, his voice puffing in and out like he was running.

"Are you freaking kidding me right now?"

"Why? Is that too early for you?" The steady thump of running footsteps traveled down the line.

"A tad," I drawled.

"And here I thought you'd be up early for the twins." His voice panted between words.

Was that how he sounded while having sex?

"Are you running?"

"I'm on the treadmill."

"Ugh." I dragged the blankets over my head to shut out the growing lightness of the sky. "What did you call for other than to wake me up and flaunt your fitness?"

He chuckled. "To invite you to my apartment tonight. I have a late business meeting and I figured it would be better if you came here."

"I'm not sleeping with you."

"Who said anything about you sleeping over?" More panting.

"Sex, then." Damn my mind for going straight to sex. To Marco pounding into me while panting like he was right now. I bet sweat covered his body too.

"I merely wanted to have you sign the amended prenuptial agreement."

"Oh. Okay. Text me the address." I toyed with the tie on my sleep shorts. "What time?"

"Ten o'clock."

"That is late." I pursed my lips.

"Unless you can get away from the kids today and come to my office?"

"No, I promised the boys I'd take them to the beach today. I'll come to your apartment tonight."

"Good girl." He panted even louder.

How hard was he running? All I pictured was him about ready to orgasm. My clit throbbed in time to his pants. Good God, how did I need another orgasm this soon after the one he'd given me last night?

"I ... ah ... have to go."

"Kennedy?" He puffed out a loud breath. "Be careful at the beach today."

My heart warmed that he cared enough to say that. He wasn't bad. We'd got off to a rocky start, but we were both good people underneath.

"I will," I said, my voice taking on a husky tone. I hung up before I said anything else. He'd said this was a marriage of convenience for him and nothing more. I couldn't let myself feel things for Marco. Nope, that'd be stupid. The man could be an asshole sometimes. I needed to remember that, but when I did, my body burned with the need for him even more.

I must be a little crazy.

A disgruntled huff left my throat. I threw back the blankets and stomped into the bathroom. With no children to watch until Mr. and Mrs. Burberry's senior's driver dropped them off at eight, I filled the bathtub and relaxed under the soothing warmth of the water and bubbles smelling like the most expensive perfume ever made. Pointless since I'd be at the beach soon and covered in sand and seawater, but what else was I to do except reach for my box of sex toys?

This was a much safer option than fantasizing my dildo was Marco's dick because that's what I'd do. Also, what I'd done for the last month since we'd stood outside William's office and listened to William and Prue have sex.

I hoped they were having a wonderful honeymoon.

Honeymoon? Why didn't I think of that? Would Marco and I have a honeymoon too? I'd ask him tonight when I saw him at his apartment. What was his apartment like? A total bachelor pad I bet. He gave off the vibe like you wouldn't catch him dead with a floral cushion in his home. I snickered, perhaps I'd insist on them in our house.

What a crazy thought. Me having a house in Beverly Hills. With a husband. My ex-boyfriend worked at Home Depot. Great aspirations and all. He'd been a real catch. Not. At least he'd shown me how awful he was when he left me. I ran a finger over the scar on my stomach, a tiny little white line you wouldn't even know was there unless you examined the spot, or I pointed it out. The place the doctors removed my fallopian tube, and the baby stuck in it. The one thing which made it almost impossible for me to have children.

I climbed out of the bath before my thoughts turned my mood dark. A day with the twins at the beach would soon brighten even the darkest of moods. I loved those kids like they were my own. At least marrying Marco I'd be more than their nanny. I'd become their surrogate aunty too.

There'd be perks to this marriage that didn't include the body-shaking orgasms the man produced without even getting in my panties.

That was what I was looking forward to the most. The life. Not the orgasms. If only my body believed me too.

**\*\*\*\***

I caught an Uber to Marco's address which he'd sent through to my cell straight after I'd hung up. The man didn't miss a beat. He'd probably be a good husband. The apartment building was massive, as I'd expected. A doorman opened the front door for me, and I walked over to the desk. Every inch of the place screamed money, from the burgundy carpeting to the gold pendant lights and the marble countertop.

"Good evening, ma'am," the concierge said. "Who is expecting you this fine evening?"

"Mr. Lawrence."

"Who may I say is calling?"

"Kennedy."

He peered down his nose at me.

"Miss Fuller."

"Very well, Miss Fuller, I'll let him know you have arrived."

"Thank you."

The concierge picked up the phone, spoke into the handpiece, then told me to head on up in the lift. Inside the lift, annoying pan pipe music played through the speaker system. I watched the numbers flash red as the lift passed each floor. Up and up, I traveled until the lift dinged at the penthouse. I should have known he'd live in the most expensive apartment.

Marco stood at his open door, his arm resting against the doorjamb in a relaxed pose. That wasn't the only thing relaxed. Instead of the immaculate suit and tie, he wore a white t-shirt and gray sweatpants. My mouth watered. The sweatpants hid nothing at all. The long shape of his cock hung down his thigh. I shuffled closer almost too afraid the trouser snake would jump out and bite me.

When in truth I wanted his trouser snake to do more than bite me.

"You look sun-kissed," Marco said.

I touched a hand to my warm cheek. "Yeah, I got a little sun today at the beach."

"I thought I told you to be careful." He leaned closer as I slid between him and the open door. "I should spank your ass for not taking better care of yourself."

I spun around. "I don't do that."

"What?" He closed the door. "Spanking?"

"Yes."

"Oh, sweetheart, I thought you'd finished with the lies."

I folded my arms over my chest. "I don't."

"Don't or haven't?"

I puffed out a breath. "Haven't and don't want to."

"Okay." He held his hands out in a peace offering. "I'll cross spanking off the list of things I plan to do to you."

"You have a list?" I dropped my arms.

He stepped closer. "A very long list."

I inhaled the clean scent of his soap and shampoo, different from his expensive aftershave, but no less alluring. Perhaps even more so. I wanted to lick him from head to foot then ask him to do the same to me. No, I wouldn't crumble this easily.

"So, this is your place?" I spun around too fast and the room blurred.

"Let me give you a tour." He placed his hand on my back between my shoulder blades.

There was nothing gentle or caring in his hold, it

was pure dominance for me to follow his way. My body recognized the control, liked it, and broke out in goose bumps.

"This is the living area."

We stopped inside the massive living room housing a flat-screen television a cinema would be proud of, a large black leather lounge suite, and a glass coffee table.

"Nice," I said.

He urged me to the next room. The kitchen. Italian marble gleamed from every countertop. High-end appliances a woman dreamed about adorned the cupboards.

"Suitable," I said, not willing to admit I was drooling over the kitchen.

Marco showed me to every room in the apartment—bedrooms, bathrooms, his office, study, piano room. I didn't know he played the piano, but his firm hand kept me moving before I could ask him to play for me.

"This is my video room."

"Don't you watch videos on the enormous television?"

"Yes." He opened the door. "This is where I make them." He flicked on the light switch.

I gasped. In the center of the room sat a queen-size bed, a mirror hung from the ceiling, and the headboard. On the sides and base of the bed stood three video cameras on tripods.

"Holy cow, you do make porn videos." I stepped into the room. His hand slid from my back. "Of yourself? And other women?"

"Yes."

I ran a hand over the video camera at the bottom of the bed then over the Egyptian cotton sheets. I sat on the bed, tilted my head up, and stared at the mirror. What would it be like to watch Marco's ass as he pounded into me? A slow smile crept onto my face.

"You're a pervert like me."

He walked into the room, adjusted the camera which I'd tilted a tiny fraction when I'd touched it, then peered at me over the top. His finger tapped against the button on the side. The on-off switch. Was he contemplating videoing me? And him? I liked the idea a lot. I ran my hands down my denim-clad thighs. Why had I worn jeans? If I'd worn a dress, I could spread my legs and tell him I was a dirty girl. If I did, would he lick me again?

"I knew this wouldn't repulse you."

"But some women are?"

"Yes. Not all, but some. I've learned to read the signs, and you give off a big flashing neon sign of being turned on by the idea."

I smoothed my damp palms down my legs again. "I am."

"It'd be easy for me to switch on the button." His finger stopped tapping.

"Then what? Would you climb on the bed with me?"

"If you asked."

I ran my fingers through my ponytail.

"That damn ponytail," he grumbled.

"What about it?"

"You look like a schoolgirl."

I laughed. "I wore pigtails at school."

He groaned.

My gaze fell to the growing snake in his sweatpants. Good God, the thing was huge. I stood from the bed and walked out of the door. I wasn't cracking first. No way. I'd show him I wasn't as easy as he thought I was.

I glanced over my shoulder. "Where's the prenuptial agreement?"

"In my office." He followed me out but left the door wide open like he was testing my resolve that I wouldn't ask him to go back in there and make a video of us.

"Let's see it, then I need to head home to bed, since some idiot woke me up too early this morning."

"Who would wake a sleeping beauty?"

"I know, right? Let's hope he's learned his lesson for married life."

He chuckled so deep and husky it ramped up my libido even more. Damn the man and his husky tone. It was almost as much of a turn-on as when he commanded me.

We sat in his office while I read through the prenuptial agreement again. Everything appeared in order. If I was rich, I'd get a lawyer to read over it, but since I wasn't, I picked up a pen and signed my name. Marco signed the contract too then placed the papers in his briefcase.

"So that's it," I said, standing.

Marco stood and walked me to his front door. "I'll come by Sunday before William and Prue get home, then we can tell them together."

"Oh, we won't see each other before then?"

"We're not dating, Kennedy, this is a marriage of convenience. Don't expect flowers and chocolates or date nights."

I glared at him. "I wouldn't even dream of it."

"Good girl."

The praise and the way he said it, had my body humming in overdrive. Asshole Marco made me a very dirty girl indeed. Didn't that make me a bad girl instead of the good girl he kept calling me? I walked over to the lift and stabbed the button with my finger.

"Feel free to call me anytime," he called out.

Yeah, I wasn't crumbling first. I stepped onto the lift and waggled my fingers as the doors shut in our faces. His smirk was the last thing I saw.

## Chapter Seven

True to his word, I didn't see Marco for the rest of the week. Half of me was thankful, the other half was irritated. William's parents dropped off the twins, Whit and Tuck. It excited them their parents were coming home today. They ran around the mansion pretending they were airplanes and making zooming noises. My head pounded. My heart beat in an erratic rhythm. Frankly, I was a bundle of nerves about telling Prue that Marco and I were getting married. Which was pathetic since Prue was one of the coolest people I knew.

Still, I worried what she'd say. I worried if she wouldn't want me as her nanny at all if I couldn't be here all the time. My stomach churned at the notion of not seeing the twins every day. I was way too attached to them.

The doorbell rang. I rushed to answer the door hoping it was Prue and William back ahead of schedule. My hopes dropped as I swung the door open to Marco.

"They're not here yet," I said.

"No shit."

"*Zoom.*" The boys flew toward the door.

"Uncle Marco, come play with us," Whit said.

"We're planes," Tuck said.

"I see." Marco stepped into the mansion and stuck his arms out, then followed the boys through the house, adding his zoom to the bedlam.

"Great," I mumbled, "just what I need, another kid making noise."

Marco flew past me. "What?"

"Nothing." I forced a smile. "Why don't you boys play planes outside where there's more room?"

"Good idea." Marco grabbed my hand and forced me to make a plane with him and flew us out the back door and around the pool deck.

After two laps, I shook my hand free and plonked myself on a sun lounger. Marco continued to chase the boys around the pool until he collapsed on the lounger next to me.

"Don't they ever stop?"

"Nope." I clapped my hands. "Boys, how about a snack?"

The mentions of snacks made them pause their flying.

"Cookies?" Whit asked.

"Okay." I stood. "I'll bring them out here."

"Milk too," Marco called out.

I threw him a surprised glance before ducking into the kitchen and getting the cookies. In usual circumstances, I wouldn't leave the boys near the pool, but Marco was there to monitor them. Which he did by getting back up and chasing them around the pool again. At least he was wearing them out.

My phone buzzed with a message from Prue saying their plane was delayed and they wouldn't be home until tonight. *Oh, no, the boys will be disappointed.* I added more cookies to the plate hoping that would cheer them up. Balancing three glasses of milk and the plate of cookies on a tray, I headed back outside. The boys rushed over to the table and sat in their chairs. Marco joined us and snatched a cookie before the boys.

"So, um, your mom messaged me, their plane is late," I said to the boys. "They won't be home until after you're in bed."

Tuck's bottom lip trembled. "But I want my mommy."

"I know you do, darling," I said. I picked him up out of his seat and cuddled him.

Whit crawled out of his seat and onto my lap too.

"I want Mommy and Daddy."

"It won't be much longer," I crooned, rubbing their backs. "I promise. When you wake up in the morning, it will be like Christmas."

"Christmas?" Whit asked.

"Ah-huh," I said. "Mommy and Daddy will have presents for you."

I'd have crossed my fingers if my hands weren't busy patting their backs.

"That's right," Marco said. "Every time my parents go on a holiday, they bring me back a present."

"They do?" Tuck squirmed off my lap and over to Marco's.

"When they traveled to Africa, they fetched me a toy lion that roared whenever I touched its back."

"I want a toy lion," Whit said, returning to his chair and picking up a biscuit.

"It'll be a surprise what they bring home," Marco said.

Tuck ate a biscuit but stayed on Marco's lap. At least it was progressing, and they weren't crying anymore.

"Who wants to swim after their biscuits?" Marco asked.

"Me," the boys chorused.

Okay, guess we were going in the pool. Me, Marco, and the twins.

Could I swim with him without checking out his body and trouser snake? I choked on my cookie. Marco handed me his glass of milk since I didn't get one for myself. I sipped the crumbs from the back of my throat and handed the milk back to Marco. He licked the edge of the glass where my lips left a mark then drank the remaining milk. Heat licked its way from the inside of my body to the outside.

"Okay." I jumped out of my seat like a shark was about to attack me. A lawyer shark if I asked him. "Let's go put our swimmers on."

The boys squealed and ran to the back door.

"You have swimmers, don't you?"

"Of course." Marco laughed. "We'll save skinny-dipping for another time."

****

After swimming, dinner of spaghetti which ended with the boys covered in red sauce, baths to clean them up, and a short children's movie, the twins were in bed asleep. I sunk onto the couch next to Marco, toed my shoes off, and sighed.

"They're exhausting," he murmured.

"Yep." I flung my feet up onto the couch, by a hair's breadth missing kicking Marco. "Thanks for your help today."

"You're welcome."

"You know, you're a good uncle. Why do you have to be an asshole too?"

He flicked my big toe with his finger. "It's who I am, besides, you like it when I'm an asshole."

I opened my mouth to deny it when the front door swung open. I scrambled up from the couch but not before Prue walked into the house.

"They're asleep," I said.

"Shit." She pouted, her entire face dropping in disappointment. "How are they?"

"Terrors," Marco said.

"Marco?" Prue's eyes widened in surprise and then she pinned him with her gaze. "Why are you here?"

William walked into the mansion and dumped their suitcases on the floor. He surveyed the scene like a king surveying his land.

"Hey." William tipped his head at Marco.

"Did you have a good honeymoon?" Marco asked.

"Cut the crap," Prue said. "What are you doing with my nanny?" She pointed her finger at Marco. "I know you, Marco, and you wouldn't be here unless you were up to something."

William laughed. "Prue, honey, I know you're disappointed we didn't make it home to see the kids before they went to bed, but you don't need to take it out on Marco."

I ran a hand through my ponytail.

"Shit." Prue stormed across the room and grabbed my hand. "What's this rock?"

"I ... ah ... we're engaged."

Prue glared at Marco but didn't let go of my hand. "Nope, not happening."

Marco placed his hands in his pockets. "It already has."

"I don't believe this for one second." She tugged me to sit with her on the couch.

"What don't you believe?"

"You two getting married."

William stepped behind the couch and massaged her shoulders. "The ring speaks for itself, Prue."

Prue flicked her gaze back and forth between Marco and me.

"All right then, explain how you two have all of a sudden decided to get married after knowing each other for years without a hint of attraction."

She was right, there'd been no attraction between us until the night outside William's office when we'd both listened to them have sex.

"It was ... ah ... your wedding." I nodded. "That's right. Your wedding renewal was so romantic and special it was like you doused us with love too, and like those moments in the movies where you look at a person and see them differently and know you're going to spend the rest of your life with them."

"Aww, that's sweet." Prue rubbed her small pregnant stomach. "Now prove it."

"Huh?"

"Kiss." She grinned and pushed my shoulder. "Get up there and kiss your fiancé. He is your fiancé, right?"

"Um, yes, he is." I lurched to my feet and made my way over to Marco. His gray eyes twinkled with amusement as I stretched up on tippy-toes and kissed his cheek. "There." I turned to Prue, triumphant.

Prue rolled her eyes.

Marco's firm hands cupped my shoulders and turned me back to face him. Gaze intent on my lips he lowered his head slowly, building the expectation. The entire atmosphere heated with anticipation. Or was it me? Closer and closer his face descended until it blurred, and I shut my eyes at the last second before his lips touched mine. Oh, my. My lips trembled, he soothed them with his lips, then caressed them with his tongue until my hands slid up his chest and clutched the lapels of his shirt. He forced his tongue through my lips making me moan with the demand in his kiss. My knees wobbled. His hands smoothed downward from my shoulders to the roundness of my butt and hauled me into the firmness of his erection. I rocked my hips against him.

William cleared his throat in a loud exaggerated manner.

I gave Marco a little shove with my palms. He released my mouth from his assertive kiss and tucked me into his side.

"Well," Prue said, fanning her face. "I can't argue with that kiss. Seriously, Kennedy, it's about time too."

My face heated. Did she have to spell it out for everyone how long it'd been since I'd had sex?

"Anyway…" I lifted my gaze to Marco's face then wriggled out of his arm and sat back next to Prue. "Can we get married at your new resort as you did?"

"Hell, yeah." Prue sat up. "I love the idea. When do you want to get married? Wait! What am I going to do for a nanny?"

I held her hand. "I'm still going to be your kids' nanny, but Marco and I were hoping you could find another nanny for the night. If you still want me to be your nanny, that is?"

Prue clutched my hand. "Of course I want you to still be our nanny. The kids adore you. I adore you. Will thinks highly of you too."

"Good." I smiled. "In three weeks, then, we'll get married."

Prue nodded. "Venue is doable for then since the resort doesn't open yet for another month. I'll call the caterers tomorrow. How many guests are we looking at?"

"From my side, about fifty." I let go of Prue's hand and waved at Marco. "What about you?"

"Better add a hundred for me to be on the safe side."

"Invitations?"

I shook my head.

"We can sort them out tomorrow too. Will, who did you use for ours?"

"I'll call the company tomorrow, then get them to call you for all the details," William said.

"Thanks." I swallowed. This was happening.

"What about a dress? Tiff can make you one."

"I … ah … have the dress sorted. I need to head home to pick it up."

Marco scowled. "You already have a wedding

dress?"

"My grandmother's."

"Ah." He looked like a scolded kid.

"Do you mind if I take next Saturday off and deliver the invitations to my family and pick up the dress?"

"Take the entire weekend," Prue said. "Marco can drive you."

"Um, yeah?"

Marco's scowl returned. "I have a phone meeting Saturday morning."

"Pfft, you can take a phone meeting in the car, as Will does. You should meet Kennedy's family before you marry her."

"Don't argue with a pregnant woman," William said. "You won't win."

"Okay." Marco shoved his hands in his pockets.

"Have you met Marco's family yet?"

"I've met them at your pool parties."

"I mean as his fiancé?"

"Well, no … I wanted to tell you first."

Prue threw her arms around my neck and hugged me. "I hope you're as happy as I am married."

"I'm sure I will be," I mumbled into her thick black hair, keeping my gaze from drifting to Marco.

He'd know I was lying, and he wouldn't like it. I didn't like it. Marco was right. I was greedy in wanting what Prue and William had. Being greedy wasn't something I ever thought I was until it stared me in the face. Was it such a terrible sin, though, to want to be happily married?

## Chapter Eight

By Wednesday, Prue was suspicious I hadn't asked for a night off to see Marco, nor had he arrived at the mansion to see me. I thumbed his number on my phone then sent him a message explaining Prue's behavior. The three dots appeared right away.

Marco: **Come over then.**

Me: **Be there soon.**

I could have gone out to a movie or something and pretended I was seeing him, but a part of me wanted to see Marco. Crazy as that was.

I found Prue in the boys' bedroom reading them a bedtime story.

"If it's okay with you, can I head out for a few hours?"

"Absolutely, have fun." She winked.

I changed into a pair of navy denim jeans and a white blouse, donned a pair of boots, and ordered an Uber. A longer drive than I preferred through the heavy evening traffic, and I arrived at Marco's city apartment building again. The concierge greeted me by name and told me to go straight on up. Guess Marco had made us official. A tiny thrill of delight sparked inside my stomach.

His penthouse suite door was open, but he wasn't lounging against the doorjamb this time. I let myself in and closed the door. Heavy metal music blared from the hidden speakers in the ceiling. I hadn't figured him to be a hard-core music fan.

"Marco?"

"In my office," he called out.

I picked my foot up then let it hover in midair. Did I interrupt him in his office or leave him be? If he wanted to see me, he would have come out and greeted me. I changed direction and walked into his kitchen, poured myself a glass of wine, after rummaging through his cupboards looking for a wineglass, because, hey, he was my fiancé after all, then sat on the kitchen counter sipping the glass. My feet swung in time to the music, it was hard not to bop along to the heavy beats of the music. I picked the bottle up and topped up my glass as the next song kicked over.

"Hey," Marco said, walking into the kitchen after who knows how long.

"Sorry about tonight."

"No problem." He opened the cupboard, drew out a wineglass, and poured the remaining wine into his bottle. "I see you like this label."

I swirled the last half of my glass. "Yeah, it's smooth."

He snorted. "It should be for a three-hundred-dollar bottle."

The glass wobbled in my hand. "Shit, I didn't know." This was awkward. We hadn't even spoken to each other since our first kiss. The one that claimed me as his fiancée. Yes, that's what he did, he'd marked himself on my lips and inside my mouth. And the dirty girl I was wanted more of it. My body hungered for him to mark all of me.

He caught my hand in his. "Don't spill the wine, otherwise I'll have to make you lick it up so you don't waste a drop."

I sucked in a breath, dropping my gaze to his bare feet under the black slacks. He'd removed his suit jacket and rolled up the sleeves of his white shirt leaving his tanned forearms on display. He'd undone the top three buttons as well. I knew all too well how sculpted his chest was, perks of Prue's pool parties. He was way too sexy. I thought about licking the wine from his feet and loving every minute.

He stroked his thumb over the back of my hand. "You're an interesting woman, Kennedy, I say the most asshole things and you get turned on by it."

"Yeah, well," I spluttered.

He tugged the glass from my hand and placed it on the shiny marble countertop. My heart rate picked up, a loud booming through my ears. He must have heard it too. What would he do next? Kiss me again? Go down on me again? This time with nothing in the way, with any luck.

"Two little words, Kennedy, that's all you have to say."

"What?" I licked my lips.

"Please, Marco," he crooned.

I snatched my glass off the counter and finished the wine. I was not asking him for sex. He sipped his drink, watching me over the rim of his glass.

"Not happening." I firmed my lips even though they wanted to utter those two words.

"Would you like to watch a movie?"

I flicked a glance at the time on my cell. I hadn't been away long enough. "Sure."

"Good girl." He walked out of the kitchen to the lounge room.

Good girl that I was, I followed him. What the hell was it with those two little words that made me eager to obey him like a fool? I launched myself at the couch, okay, I was tipsy and I may have stumbled, but I made it appear as though I'd intentionally meant to sprawl along the leather. Marco peered over his shoulder, his gray eyes sparkling with amusement. He punched numbers into a locked box on top of the entertainment unit and withdrew a USB stick, plugged it into the side of the giant television, then sat on the couch near me.

The screen flicked on asking for another pass code.

"Anyone would think you're a spy." I rolled my eyes.

Marco tapped on his phone. "Who says I'm not?"

The heavy metal music volume lowered before the unmistakable sounds of sex erupted from the screen.

"I know I said I'd show you after we're married, but…" He rolled his shirt-clad shoulders.

I sat up and leaned forward. "Is that you?"

"I sure as shit don't video other guys having sex."

I tilted my head sideways as the Marco on the television rearranged the woman's position on the screen. He was now having sex with her side-on instead of doggy style like they'd started. The woman arched her back like she loved every second Marco thrust into her. Her breasts bounced every time his pelvis slammed into her ass.

"Are you…?" I inched closer until I sat on the edge of the couch.

On the screen Marco lifted the woman's leg leaving the view of the camera wide open to the sight of his cock thrusting into the woman's vagina.

"Am I what?" Marco's voice came out rough.

"Never mind, I can see the angle now."

He chuckled. "You were wondering if I was in her ass?"

I nodded, too transfixed with the images on the television. Holy hotness, my clit throbbed against the seam of my jeans. Why had I worn jeans? If I'd worn a dress, I could have slipped my hand underneath and got off from this video.

"Have you done that, Kennedy?" Marco's voice sounded next to my ear.

I bit my lip and nodded.

"Such a dirty girl."

I turned my head to face the real Marco, not the sex stud on the screen, and boy, was he a stud. My entire body was heated, about to burst into flames. Marco's hand rubbed up and down the impressive bulge in his pants. I stared at him in fascination. Would he come like that? Or would he take out his cock and then come? I very much wanted to see it. See him in the flesh.

The woman on the screen screamed. Guess she'd achieved her climax. Not like me. I was nowhere near it, nor Marco by the way his hand kept stroking his pants. His hand captivated me, but what he had underneath lured me. I wanted to wrench his hand away and climb on his lap.

I shut my eyes and huffed. I. Would. Not. Ask. Him.

Blinking open my eyes, I stood in a rush. "Thanks for the wine, and the…" I waved my hand at the screen but didn't stare at it, because if I did then I'd see Marco come, and if I saw his pleasure then I'd want to experience it in real life. Like right now. Inside me. "I'll … ah … I'm going."

"Not coming?" He smirked.

"Screw you." I stomped over to the front door.

He caught up to me and got his hand on the doorknob before me. "Say pretty please, Marco, screw me, and I will."

I spun around. "You're freaking funny, aren't you?"

My chest heaved with every word, drawing his expensive aftershave in deeper and making my insides clench with need.

"Glad you see it, fiancée."

I glowered. How had I ever agreed to marry him? Oh, right, he'd blackmailed then I'd kind of felt sorry for him. Plus, he'd always been a nice guy until now. I yanked my phone out of my back pocket and ordered an Uber.

"Oh, goody, the Uber is two minutes away."

"I would have driven you home."

"With your crazy driving, no, thanks." I tapped his hand on the doorknob. "You can open the door now."

He opened the door for me all gentlemanlike. "Good night, Kennedy. Thanks for coming, oh, wait, you didn't."

"Neither did you."

He dropped his hand to his pants and the still hard erection straining at the fabric. "I will be sooner than you."

"Good for you," I spat and stormed to the lift, stabbing the button with my finger.

"Oh, and Kennedy, I'll pick you up at seven o'clock Saturday morning, then we'll be at your parents' place before lunch."

The lift dinged and the doors slid open with a quiet hiss.

"Okay, I'll let them know," I said, climbing inside.

Instead of being turned on, I was now a bundle of anxious nerves because my parents would see right through this farce of an engagement.

## Chapter Nine

Saturday morning arrived too soon. I'd taken the "chicken" route and texted my sister to tell Mom and Dad I'd be home for lunch on Saturday. Zara being Zara called me the instant she received the message demanding to know what was going on. I'd kept my lips tight and told her she'd find out Saturday. That way at least she'd be there as a buffer. No doubt she wouldn't make a difference, but I had to try.

Marco's Camaro rumbled into the driveway of the Burberry mansion and since I was already waiting outside, I jumped into the seat before he even switched off the engine.

"Bit eager, are we?"

"No, I didn't want to wake everyone." I crossed my arms over my chest.

"Nice dress," he said, driving the car back onto the road.

"Um, thanks?"

"I meant it." He frowned. "Let's try to be nice to each other today, okay?"

"Sure." I uncrossed my arms.

"Who am I meeting today?" He weaved the car through the heavy morning traffic.

I grabbed hold of the sides of the seat. "My mom, Dianne, Dad, Rick, sister, Zara. My brother Elijah is away at college, he's going to be the next biggest ballplayer."

"Baseball?"

"Yep."

"Dad's a huge Arizona Diamondbacks fan. He'll be super proud if Elijah gets on the team."

"The Los Angeles Dodgers are a better team, he'd be better off in LA."

"That might be true, but never say that to Dad."

"Right, no talking about baseball. Anything else?"

"You might want to slow down." I dug my fingernails into the leather seats.

"There's nothing wrong with my driving."

He sped the car through a narrow gap in the traffic and zoomed ahead of a truck. I shook my head.

"How old are you again?"

"Forty-three, why?"

"You drive like a teenager."

"And you can drive better?"

"I can. Pull over and I'll show you."

"You're not driving my car," he said like every man ever about his prized possession.

"Fine." I huffed. "Have it your way, don't say I didn't tell you to slow down."

"Kennedy..." He sighed my name like I was the one causing problems. "My meeting starts soon, there's a pair of noise-canceling headphones in the glove box."

"Is that your way of asking me to wear them?"

"Can you please wear the headphones? The meeting will have confidential information."

"Sure, I'll connect them to my reading app." I opened the glove box and fished out the fanciest headphones I'd ever used. "These must have set you back a bit." I snapped them over my ears and flicked through my phone, set the device to an audiobook, then gave Marco a thumbs-up.

He smiled and mouthed *good girl*. I swung my gaze out the side window and settled back to listen to the romance story. Or more accurately porn. Every time the narrator reached the part where the couple was having sex my gaze flicked to Marco's lap. To the draw of his suit pants over his thighs and bulge at his crotch. He wasn't as impressive as he'd been the other night while his video had been playing, but still...

Marco tapped my chin.

I met his sparkling gray gaze. He had such pretty eyes. Pity about his attitude sometimes. He smirked, then returned to talking over the Bluetooth system. How long was his meeting? We'd been in the car for four hours. Not much further and then we'd be in my hometown. All being well, this book would be finished by the time we arrived. I liked to get to the happy ending. They more often than not comprised a big sex scene too at the end. I pointed at the dashboard and the speedometer. Marco shook his head and ignored my silent request for him to slow down.

*Fool.*

A nervous bubble rolled around in my stomach. I hadn't seen my parents for a couple of months. They were bound to be all over this engagement and marriage since if Marco and I had been dating, I would have at least mentioned him. I would have at least said I was bringing him with me this weekend.

Chicken noises drowned out the narrator as my brain squawked them at me. I hit "pause" and tapped Marco's shoulder. He glanced my way, and I pointed at my headphones. He held up a finger, his mouth flapped more before he hit a button on his steering wheel and nodded. I lifted the headphones. The silence in the car was strange.

"We're not far now," I said.

"I have the navigation system on," he said like it was obvious he knew we weren't far from my parents' house.

"You might want to slow down."

"Are you nagging me already and we're not even married yet?"

"Have you ever been to Arizona?"

"No, why?"

"Don't say I didn't warn you."

As if I'd summoned them, red and blue police lights flashed along with the distinctive wail of the siren. Marco peered in his rearview mirror, cursed under his breath, and pulled the car over to the side of the road. I didn't say I told you so, but I wanted to.

The police officer knocked on the window. Marco wound it down.

"License and registration, please," the officer said.

I sucked in a breath, leaned over Marco's shoulder, and said, "Hi, Daddy."

Dad ducked lower and peered into the car, the surprise clear on his face as he said, "Kennedy?"

"Yep."

Dad's surprise vanished, and he narrowed his eyes. "What are you doing in this asshole's car?"

"Wait a minute," Marco spluttered.

I placed my left hand on Marco's chest. "He's my fiancé."

"Are you shitting me?" Dad peered closer at Marco.

"Nope."

"Well, then," Dad drawled. "Care to explain why you were speeding with my daughter in your car?"

"I, ah..." Marco flicked his gaze to me then met my dad's glare. "No excuse."

"Right answer, dickwad. Don't do it again." He held his hand out.

Marco placed his papers in Dad's hand and watched him write up a ticket. My chest shook while trying to hold in my laughter.

"I'm heading back to the station to clock off, then

I'll see you both at home." He tapped the roof of the car. "Drive carefully. It'd be a real shame if I had to impound this beauty."

Marco ground his teeth.

"See you soon, Daddy."

Dad strutted back to his Harley-Davidson Road King, revved the throttle on the motorbike, then sped off.

"So, it's all right for your dad to speed?" Marco grumbled.

"He's not speeding, he takes off fast."

Marco clicked a button and his phone sounded back through the Bluetooth system.

"Sorry, Angus, I need to finish the call now."

"We'll talk about this more Monday morning."

He ended the call leaving us listening to the loud beeping of the dial tone.

"Your dad is a cop. A little heads-up would have been good before he wrote me a ticket."

I let the giggle I'd been holding out.

"Come on," I said, "it's funny."

His lips twitched as he shook his head. "What else do I need to know before I meet your family?"

"Took you long enough to ask." I twirled the headphones in my hands. "Dad is a cop, he's a no-nonsense sort of guy. Don't think you can sweet-talk him with your fancy lawyer negotiations."

"I already figured that out."

I laughed again. "Mom is a school counselor, she's worse than Dad. She sees right through bullshit."

"What the hell, Kennedy?"

"What?" I shrugged. "You wanted to blackmail me into marrying you, it's the least I could do to pay you back."

"I thought you were marrying me to help me out now, since you kind of like me."

I snorted. "Don't kid yourself. I see how good you are with the Burberrys and that is the reason I'm helping you."

He turned the car into my home street.

"I think you're the one kidding yourself now." He tapped buttons on the steering wheel and my audiobook exploded through the speakers.

*"He thrust his hard cock into her willing flesh."*

"No, no, no." I scrambled with my phone and turned off the book.

Marco laughed. "We can listen to the end on the way back home later."

I gathered up my tote bag as Marco drove the car up to my parents' driveway and shoved the phone inside.

"I'm interested to know how the story ends."

"Shut up." I glowered.

"But, Kennedy, we're about to meet your parents as a happily engaged couple, this is perfect. You can think of me thrusting into—"

I slammed a hand over his mouth.

His gray eyes darkened into blazing steel.

"You can try to pretend we're a happy couple in front of my parents, but it won't work."

He pried my fingers from over his lips. "Why are we here then?"

"The dress, silly. It's all about the dress."

## Chapter Ten

I knocked on the front door with damp, sweaty palms. Marco stood next to me, a half-grimace, half-smile on his face. The poor guy looked constipated. Mom opened the door and smiled an I-know-everything smile.

"Dad called you," I said, stepping inside and kissing her cheek.

"Of course." She held out her hand. "You must be Marco, my daughter's fiancé. I'm Dianne."

"Pleasure to meet you, Dianne." Marco shook her hand and followed me into the house. "Lovely home you have here in Arizona."

"Thank you. We like it here. It's a shame Kennedy ran off to a different state."

"Mom," I scolded.

"Well, you did, dear, after the fool you were dating left you in the hospital."

Unexpected pain surged through my body. I was over my ex-boyfriend but what he did still hurt like the pain of the ectopic pregnancy in my stomach.

"Did he hurt you?" Marco stepped closer to me.

I firmed my lips and shook my head.

"If he physically hurt you, you need to tell me." Marco placed his hands on my shoulders and stared into my face.

"It wasn't like that."

His tense grip loosened a fraction, but he didn't let me go. "What happened?"

"He, ah, I … well … we got pregnant, and it wasn't right. I had an ectopic pregnancy and needed surgery to remove it."

Every muscle in his face softened as sympathy washed over him. "I'm sorry." He drew me into his chest and hugged me.

Well, this was nice. I buried my nose into his suit jacket and inhaled his expensive aftershave, but underneath was the masculine scent unique to Marco. He rubbed my back with firm yet gentle strokes, sending my body into hyper-awareness of how close we were. Of the intimacy of the embrace. How much I liked it.

I cleared my throat and stepped back.

"He broke up with me when I got out of surgery, said he was glad I lost the baby because he couldn't imagine being with me his whole life."

His fingers curled into tight fists. "What's his name? Where does he live?"

"You're like her dad," Mom said and patted Marco on the back of his shoulder.

*Holy crap, he wasn't, was he?*

"Rick made his life hell for months, still does whenever he can find something to give him a ticket for." She laughed. "The poor guy had his car impounded, he had that many fines."

Dad walked through the front door as Mom finished talking.

"And he deserved every one of those fines," Dad said. "I don't make them up."

"Of course you don't, dear." Mom slid into Dad's side like they were magnets compelled to be together. "What's this all about?"

"Can we at least have a drink? Even lunch before you analyze me?"

Mom smiled. "Yes, your sister should be here any minute since you told her you were coming."

"That's all I told her," I huffed.

"Come on outside to the deck. Your dad is going to grill meat on the barbeque, and he's made his famous hot sauce."

"Great." I licked my lips. Dad's hot sauce was

worth coming home for.

"Do you like hot sauce?" Mom asked Marco.

"Can't say I've tried it," he said.

"Be prepared to have your taste buds dazzled."

We followed Mom to the deck while Dad ducked upstairs to change out of his uniform. Mom made small talk about the weather in Arizona compared to Los Angeles while we waited. Zara bounced around the back of the house, her long blonde hair flying with each happy step.

"What's up?" She plonked into the chair beside me. "Who's this?"

"I'm engaged. This is Marco, my fiancé, and we're getting married in two weeks."

"Like hell you are," Dad said joining us.

"Daddy, I don't need your permission to get married."

Dad scowled and stalked to the grill where he donned his apron and slapped the meat on the hot plate Mom had already preheated.

"Zara, would you be my bridesmaid?"

"Can I pick my dress?"

"Go for it."

"Deal." She faced Marco and held out her hand. "Hi. I'll be your new sister-in-law."

"Hello." Marco shook her hand and took her in. "What do you do for a living?"

"Didn't Kennedy tell you?"

"No, I'm afraid she hasn't told me much about any of you."

"That'd be Kennedy." Zara picked up a napkin and ripped it to pieces. "She always likes to keep things to herself. I'm a therapist. I followed in Mom's shrink steps."

"You don't look old enough."

"Spot on. I recently graduated and I'm looking for a job. Technically, I'm not anything."

Marco smiled.

"But I plan on using my degree, not like Kennedy."

Marco turned to me with a questioning lift of his eyebrow. "You have a degree?"

"You're marrying him? Does he even know anything about you?" Zara shot me a glare. "Kennedy has a teaching degree."

"Explains why you're so good with the twins."

"How are the twins?" Mom asked.

"They're great." I tugged out my phone and showed Mom and Zara recent photos.

"They're big now," Mom said.

"I know. I can't wait for Prue to have her baby and I can hold a little one again," I said.

A sad expression flittered over Mom's face. It was never far from her mind that I could have had a baby too, a child about the same age as Prue's twins if my pregnancy had gone right instead of wrong.

Marco slid his hand to the back of my neck and massaged the tense muscles at the base of my skull where the pressure built almost to the point of a headache.

"You can see the twins when you come to LA for our wedding in two weeks."

"What's the rush?" Mom asked.

"We, ah, well, Prue and William's vow renewal made us see what we could have too."

Mom cocked her head and took us in. I glanced away from her and over to Dad, who grilled the meat while listening to our conversation.

"If you're looking for a younger woman to have your children, then you should choose someone other than Kennedy," Mom said.

Marco's fingers dug deeper into my neck. "That's not what this is about."

"Then what is it about? Because if my daughter was in love, she would have told us before now. Something else is going on."

"Mrs. Fuller." Marco slid his hand from my neck and leaned on the table. "Your daughter and I may not be in love, but we have a high opinion of each other. Marriage doesn't have to be about love, it's about respect, security, dependability. All those things I can offer your daughter."

Mom dropped her gaze to the table. "Marriage without love, I don't see it ending well."

"It won't end. I believe marriage is for life," Marco said.

Dad slammed the tray of meat on the table.

"Food's up," he said.

Silence descended as we piled our plates with food. Emotions clogged my throat. How would I eat one bite let alone the plateful I'd filled? Marco slid his hand onto my thigh and squeezed it. I peeked at him in shock. How was he reading my moods so well?

Dad sat in his chair at the head of the table. "How old are you, Marco?"

"Forty-three."

"And what do you do for a living?"

"I'm a lawyer."

"What type?"

"Corporate." Marco stabbed a chunk of meat and placed it in his mouth, chewed, then swallowed. "This is delicious."

Dad dipped his head.

"Are you from Los Angeles?"

"Yes, born and raised there. My mom is a plastic

surgeon, Dad is a lawyer too but works in patents. I have three brothers, all married with children."

"Wealthy, huh?"

"We do all right."

I snorted. Everyone's eyes focused on me. I dropped my gaze to my plate.

"You appear to be doing all right with this waterfront house," Marco said.

"We do all right," Dad said.

Zara snickered. I kicked her ankle under the table.

"Ow," she screeched as if I'd hurt her instead of grazing the side of her leg.

I rolled my eyes. "How's your boyfriend? What was his name?"

I couldn't remember, she changed her boyfriends like I changed my sheets.

"Julio. We broke up."

"What excuse did you use this time?"

"I'll have you know that I in fact … couldn't think of one." She laughed. "He was cool and agreed we shouldn't be dating."

Somehow her confession broke the tension around the table and the entire atmosphere changed. Dad and Marco talked law stuff while Zara, Mom, and I discussed the wedding plans. The more I talked, the more excited they were about the wedding, and me to an extent. We finished the food, consumed more drinks, and Dad produced a pack of cards.

"We should get going," Marco said.

Dad placed his palms on the table. "I counted how many drinks you had, you're over the limit to drive now."

I laughed at Marco's shocked face, picked up my wineglass, and tipped it his way. They'd lured him into a trap, one of his makings to start with. I didn't feel sorry for Marco one bit he was now stuck in Arizona with me and my family.

"And there'll be no sharing a bed with my daughter tonight," Dad said. "You'll sleep in the spare bedroom, Marco."

Marco grinned like it was the funniest thing he'd ever heard. "No problem at all, Officer Fuller."

"The name's Rick. I suppose you should call me by my name since you're marrying my daughter."

****

Much later that night after more wine and losing the card game to Zara, I led Marco to the spare bedroom downstairs. An entire floor would separate us. Dad may as well have told Marco to sleep outside.

"You're enjoying this, aren't you?" Marco said, stepping into the bedroom.

I followed him in and shut the door behind me. "I am."

"So many layers," he muttered.

"Like an onion." I giggled.

"Like one of those cakes you like to eat." He sat on the bed leaving my crotch level with his face. "The sweet icing on the outside. The moist cake on the inside. And the surprising filling hidden in the middle. I was looking forward to eating you before but now I'm ravenous for a taste." He placed his hands on my waist and tugged me closer.

My legs, of course, shifted on their own accord. He inched the hem of my dress up my thighs.

"Are you a good girl or a dirty girl?"

I scanned the room at all my parents' belongings. We shouldn't do this here. I had many dirty thoughts about Marco and his face, like grinding myself into it.

"I'm a dirty girl," I whispered.

He let my dress drop back down and released my

waist. "Go on up to your bed, Kennedy."

"Screw you." I flounced to the door.

"Soon," he said in that deep husky tone that made me all hot and bothered as I opened the door and slid through the gap.

Soon wasn't soon enough, but I'd hold out until our wedding night. I'd gone three years without sex, what was two more weeks?

## Chapter Eleven

Dad slapped a large yellow folder into my arms.

"What's this?" I asked, even though I knew what it was.

"I ran a check on your fiancé." He ground out the last word like he had rubble in his mouth.

"Thanks, Daddy." I stretched up on tippy-toes and kissed his cheek.

"You drive nice and slow back to Los Angeles." Dad tipped his head at Marco.

"I've learned my lesson," Marco said, looking way too sexy in his rumpled suit.

Did he sleep in it? Or naked?

"Bye, Mom." I hugged her then gathered up the garment bag holding Grandma's wedding dress.

"I'm still not sure about you wearing Grandma's dress, it'll be too long," Mom said, reaching for the bag.

"It's fine. Prue's best friend is a designer, she'll be able to take up the dress with no trouble."

"She can't cut the material though. Your cousins are taller than you and they might want to wear it."

"I doubt it," I said, thinking about my snobby cousins who'd never worn hand-me-downs in their lives. I bet Marco hadn't either. "But no, I won't let her cut anything. Okay?"

"Okay, okay. Go on then, get out of here and we'll see you in two weeks."

"Yep, I'll be the one in ivory."

Mom smiled. "I still can't believe it."

I walked out the door before I told her I couldn't believe it either. I'd ruin the whole mellow mood we'd slipped into with cards and drinks. Marco opened the car door for me, and I laid the dress carefully across the backseat, before settling into the passenger seat. He drove off at the slowest speed I'd ever seen from him.

"You know my grandma's scooter goes faster than this."

"Very funny," he drawled. "I'm going slow while your dad is still watching."

"You're lucky he's not on duty, he would have followed you out of the state."

"He doesn't pull his punches, does he?"

"Nope." I opened the folder.

"Kennedy, wait…"

But I'd already read the first line.

"You were engaged?"

Why did Marco having been engaged to someone else seem like a horrible thing? He was older. He could have even been married, and I hadn't asked. I scanned the paper and sat back with a sigh of relief when there was no mention of marriage.

"Yes," Marco grumbled. "It didn't end well."

Five years with the woman, engaged for four. Wow, okay, they had a long engagement. Did one of them not want to get married?

"Why the long engagement?"

"Tasha was…" He curled his fingers around the steering wheel. "She…"

"Hang on, I'll read it."

"Shut the folder. I'll tell you."

I closed the folder and waited with my hands in my lap.

"Tasha is a supermodel. She was always flying off on a photo shoot or runway somewhere, we dated for a year, then I popped the question. She said yes but she could never seem to take the time out of her schedule to fit in a wedding." He turned onto the highway and sped up the car.

A minute ticked by, and I thought he wouldn't

say anything else.

"Then she got pregnant." His jaw clenched.

"But I thought you said…?"

"Precisely." His teeth clicked, he clenched them that hard. "She said the baby was mine, and it was a miracle." He sped the car up more. "I made her get a paternity test as soon as she could. No shock to find out the baby wasn't mine."

"So, you broke up?"

He swung his head my way. "Of course, I wouldn't stay with a cheating liar."

I frowned.

"What?"

"But you loved her?"

"How do you know?"

"You wouldn't still be this angry if you didn't, maybe you still do," I said, sitting up in my seat. "That's what this is all about, isn't it? You still love your ex-girlfriend and that's why you want a marriage of convenience."

"I don't love her anymore."

"No?" I opened the folder. If he didn't love her anymore then why did he want a marriage without love?

"Kennedy, be a good girl and close the damn folder."

"Nope, not this time." I flicked the page over. "Oh, look, there are photos of you and her. Aww, didn't you make a beautiful couple?"

"Don't make me pull over."

I waved a photo. "But you look in love," I drawled. Sharp claws dug into my chest that they did indeed appear to be in love. What would it be like to have someone gaze at me like I was the one woman on the planet they couldn't live without? To have Marco look at me as though he loved me.

"Enough." He flicked on the indicator, pulled into the side lane, and stopped the car. "Give me the envelope."

"Nope." I held the papers above my head.

"You're acting like a brat." He stretched up and plucked the folder from my hands with ease. His chest brushed against mine in the process and my nipples hardened at the brief contact.

"Not fair, your arms are longer than mine," I whined to cover my instant arousal.

He tossed the folder onto the backseat. "Leave it there and put one of your books on through the Bluetooth."

"What?"

"You heard me."

"But?"

"What?" He raised an eyebrow. "Are you close to asking me for sex and don't want to be pushed even closer by listening to it?"

I yanked my phone out and picked the dirtiest book on my device.

"Not even close," I huffed.

He restarted the car and merged back into the traffic.

Four hours later, lots of sideways glances at each other and not a single word, and Marco dropped me off at the Burberry mansion. He carried the garment bag to the door and waited all gentlemanlike while I keyed in the code. We walked into the sounds of Prue and William having sex.

"You've got to be kidding me," I muttered.

Marco handed me the dress and kissed my cheek. "You're so close I can taste victory now."

"Yeah? You're even closer." I dropped my gaze to his bulging pants.

We stared at each other in an impasse. Our chests heaving. Our gazes locked. Heat and tension blazing between us. Somewhere in the mansion, Prue screamed her orgasm snapping me out of my frozen state.

"Bye. Shut the door on your way out."

"Don't worry, Kennedy, victory will taste like your pussy. It's a win for you too." He strutted to the front door and closed it behind him.

Damn the man for making me check out his butt on his way out.

"You're back," Prue said, bouncing down the stairs a few minutes later because I'd stood there in a daze imagining Marco tasting me.

"I am." I jerked back to the present. "Where are the twins?"

"Napping." Prue grinned. "We wore them out at the playground this morning. Is that the dress?"

"It is." I held up the garment bag. "Do you want to see it?"

"Right this second, what are you waiting for?"

I unzipped the bag and eased the gown free from the protection. Ivory chiffon puffed out of the bag, and the appliqué bodice shimmered in the sunlight streaming through the windows.

Prue brushed a finger over the delicate chiffon sleeves and ran her thumb over the pearl buttons that would fasten around my wrist.

"It's pretty. You'll look like a princess. I want to see you in the dress now." She shooed me toward the guest bedroom downstairs. "Go put it on. I'm calling Tiff, she'll want to see this vintage gown."

"I need her to take it up too. Do you think she'd mind?"

"No. I'll tell her to bring pins and whatever else she needs."

"Thanks, Prue. I'm lucky you found me that day."

Prue's eyes glistened. "*I* was lucky to find you." She placed a hand on her baby bump. "I'm going to miss having you here all the time."

"I'll still be here during the day," I reminded her, but I'd miss being here all the time too.

She whipped out her phone and called Tiff. After she'd filled her in on the dress situation, she hung up and said Tiff would be here soon. I disappeared into the guest bedroom, which was still set up as a massive change room from Prue's wedding. Quite handy. I hung the gown up, stood back, and took in the ivory material. I was about to get married to a man who'd blackmailed me, infuriated me, and made me experience a range of emotions. But while he might be an asshole, I liked that side of him as much as the kind side he'd displayed.

*Did I actually like Marco?*

I put on the wedding dress. The old family photos didn't do the gown justice. It was spectacular, a soft ivory material fitting snuggly across my chest, tucked in at the waist, and flared to a full skirt. I slid the pearl buttons into the loops at my wrists. The chiffon sleeves highlighted my tanned skin underneath. I buttoned up as many pearl buttons on my back as I could then creaked open the door.

"Prue, I need help with the buttons."

Prue and Tiff rushed down the hallway and squealed when they saw me.

"Gorgeous," Tiff gushed. "Turn around, let me do up the buttons."

I turned around and Tiff made quick work of the buttons.

"I wish I could make something this stunning," Tiff said.

"You've made heaps of beautiful dresses," I said.

"Yes, but this is a work of art." She fluffed the layers of the skirt. "Are you wearing heels?"

"I suppose."

"Good, heels will lift the skirt more. I won't need to take the material up as much."

"You can't cut it."

"I wouldn't dare." She gasped and bent to the floor. "Prue, can you get her heels?"

"I'm not sure I have any suitable."

"Oh, wear mine," Prue said, hurrying out of the room.

My eyes bulged. I couldn't wear her wedding shoes. She wore them all the time when having sex with William.

Tiff laughed at my expression.

"Try them on for height and you can buy your own pair," she said.

They were pretty shoes with killer heels.

"Thanks for helping with the dress."

"My pleasure," Tiff said.

"How are things with Dex and Dieter?"

There was a time not that long ago when she'd stayed here after Dieter broke up with her, but it'd been short-lived, and they were all together now.

"Fantastic." She fiddled with the hem of the dress. "We're still looking for a house we all like. Who would have thought that'd be this hard?"

Prue walked back into the room dangling the heels from her finger. She passed them to me, and I slid them on. They were a perfect fit.

"Where did you get them from, so I can buy a pair?"

"You won't be able to buy them now." She plonked herself on the bed. "They can be your 'something borrowed' for the wedding."

"Oh, I'll make you blue underwear for 'something blue'," Tiff said.

"And your dress is 'something old'," Prue said.

"So, you'll need 'something new'," Tiff said, placing pins in the hem of the dress. "Do you have a veil?"

"No, and I don't want one."

"A tiara then?" Tiff asked. "That would go well with this gown."

"Totally." Prue kicked her feet up on the bed. "A real princess then. Marco won't know what hit him when he sees you walking down the aisle."

"Mmm-hmm."

What would Marco think? Probably nothing since this was a marriage of convenience. But a tiny flutter of excitement flapped into existence inside my chest. Would he like it? Think I'm a beautiful princess?

"How did your weekend go with your family?" Prue asked.

I snickered and told them the story of Dad giving Marco a ticket and making us sleep in separate rooms. If I pretended hard enough, this moment here could almost be real and my wedding would be genuine. I'd be the lucky bride.

If it was real, then we'd be in love and we most definitely weren't.

"Prue, would you be my matron of honor?"

"Eek, hell, yes." Prue scrambled from the bed and hugged me.

"The pins," Tiff muttered.

"Ow," I grumbled as a pin pricked my leg.

"Don't bleed on the dress," Tiff shrieked.

Prue and I giggled.

William knocked on the door and entered with the twins. He took in the scene and his lips spread into a slow smile.

"You make a gorgeous bride, Kennedy," William said. "Marco will…" He shook his head and herded the boys out of the room. "Never mind."

I stared after William. Marco would what?

## Chapter Twelve

I invited myself to Maro's apartment again on Wednesday night. This time he wasn't working in his office, he wore running shorts and a tank top, and was covered in a fine sheen of glistening sweat.

My tongue swiped across the inside of my teeth like I wanted to lick him.

"The, um, the caterer is all booked." I followed him into the kitchen staring at his tight butt the entire way.

He stopped at the fridge and sculled a bottle of water. Even watching him drink turned me on. I leaned against the countertop a safe distance from him.

"My family have responded and are all staying at the resort."

He threw the empty bottle into the trash can.

"Have you heard from your family?"

He searched my face with his gaze.

"What? Do I have something on my face?"

"No."

"So, your family?"

"Yes, they're coming, but they'd like to meet you this weekend."

"Oh, okay, I can do that."

"That easy?"

"Well, yes, it makes sense, right? You met my family. I should meet yours before the big day."

He grimaced.

"Don't you want me to meet them?"

"It's not that, it's … I'm thinking this was a bad idea."

My heart kicked against my rib cage.

"If you want to call the wedding off, do it," I said, my throat so thick the words almost didn't come out.

He thrust a hand through his damp hair. "It might be for the best."

"Okay," I whispered. I spun so fast the room whirled.

Marco was there in an instant, hands on my shoulders keeping me from falling over.

"Are you all right? You looked like you were about to pass out."

"I'm okay." I wriggled in his hold, but he didn't let go and I inhaled his masculine sweaty scent. My body surged with a sudden need for the man.

His gaze dropped to my heaving chest and the hard points of my nipples.

"Forget what I said," he mumbled.

"About?" I blinked to clear the haze of desire, but it didn't work.

"We're getting married and that's it. No more negotiations."

"Okay," I whispered.

"Good girl," he said, then his lips landed on mine.

We both froze. Lips against lips. What the hell was this? A kiss or not? I slammed my eyes shut against the glare of his gray eyes. Did he want me to make the first move? Kiss him? Open my mouth and thrust my tongue inside his? Because that's what I wanted to do.

But I didn't.

We stood there for agonizing seconds. Neither of us was willing to do anything or end this standoff.

My phone buzzed in my back pocket.

We jumped apart, and I wrenched out my phone and checked the notification.

"The band confirmed," I said to clear the tension in the air.

"What sort of band?" His eyebrows dipped into a frown.

"It's a surprise for you." I grinned.

"Not some boy band or girly shit, is it? Or heaven forbid jazz?" His lip curled up into a grimace.

"Ha, you shouldn't have left the wedding planning to me." I stepped over to the fridge and took out a can of soda, any excuse to move away from him and put distance between us and the weird kiss that'd come out of nowhere and was not even an actual kiss.

"What else do I need to know about this wedding of ours?"

"We're having pastel-pink peonies."

"What are those?"

"Flowers. Expensive ones."

"Planning on making me pay big for this wedding?"

"Well, you blackmailed me into it." I hopped up onto the countertop and swung my legs.

"Negotiated."

I waved my hand. "So, what is your family like?"

"No way." He smirked. "You let me go in blind to meet your family, as if I'd give you information about my family."

"Come on, that was your fault for not asking first. At least I'm asking."

"You've met them before anyway at Prue's pool parties."

"Not the same as being your fiancée."

"I guess." He folded his arms over his sweaty chest. "I don't know, they're my family, they're all nice to me."

I snorted. "So, they don't see your asshole side?"

"No, I reserve that for work and special people."

I placed a hand on my chest. "Are you saying I'm special?"

He shook his head. "Kennedy, you'd have to be

for me to consider having you as my wife."

"Wife of convenience. Don't forget that."

"How could I? They're my terms, but it doesn't mean we can't have a little fun while married."

"We're having lots of fun already." I sipped the soda.

"We could have much more if you'd ask." He stepped closer until my feet nudged him on every swing back and forth.

"Here." I held the bottle out. "Looks like you need to cool off, you're all sweaty."

He wrapped his firm fingers around the bottle trapping mine underneath his, lifted the bottle to his lips, and drank.

"You like me sweaty." His voice dropped to that deep husky tone that sent a shiver down my spine. "You want me to make you sweaty too."

My feet stopped swinging. He stepped closer until our legs grazed.

"Say the words and I'll make you a very dirty, sweaty girl."

I slid off the countertop, my chest brushed against his on the way down. The masculine scent of his sweat invaded my senses even more, but I tilted my chin up with more steel than was inside me and met his gaze. I wouldn't ask him, as much as I wanted to.

"When are you picking me up to meet your parents?"

His jaw clenched. "Saturday, seven o'clock, for dinner. Wear something sweet and demure."

I crossed my arms. "You're telling me what to wear?"

"Wear something sexy if you want them to compare you to my supermodel ex-fiancée."

I narrowed my eyes. "Screw you."

He cupped the back of my head and lowered his mouth to my ear. "You will."

Goose bumps exploded along my skin. His palm molded to my skull and kept me a prisoner. His prisoner. And I didn't want him to let me go.

But he did.

The instant his hold dropped I stepped back.

"I'm showering," he said. "You can join me if you like or let yourself out." He stripped the tank top over his head.

Miles upon miles of rock-hard abs glistened. I stared for way too long then backed up out of the room and fled his apartment before my will crumbled even further.

Chicken sounds once more clucked inside my head.

\*\*\*\*

"Mom, Dad, this is Kennedy," Marco introduced me to his parents at their estate. "Kennedy, this is Rachael and Joseph."

Yep, an entire estate including a mansion, pool, pool house, manicured gardens of at least a hectare, and a guesthouse.

"Lovely to meet you," Rachael said, kissing both my cheeks.

"Are you even old enough to get married?" Joseph asked.

I'd worn a sweet floral floor-length dress that made me appear younger than I was. Most of my clothes were on the younger side.

"I'm twenty-nine."

"Lucky you," Rachael said. "I have clients who'd kill to have your looks or pay me a small fortune to achieve them." She laughed. "I suppose if everyone was like you, I'd be out of business."

"I can see the appeal of a younger woman," Joseph said.

Rachael tenderly backhanded her husband across the chest. He clutched her hand and kissed it.

"My dear, don't harm the moneymakers."

She laughed. "You're such a scallywag."

"It's why you love me."

She swooned into his arms. Literally. Like a scene from a movie. They were adorable and clearly loved each other. Why didn't Marco want a relationship like theirs for himself?

"Come on into the dining room, your brothers are all here too," Rachael said.

Marco placed his hand on my lower back and escorted me into the large dining room housing a marble table seating a dozen black leather chairs. They introduced me to his two brothers, their wives, and their many children. I didn't realize he came from a big family. And they were wonderful, open and honest. Caring too. Throughout dinner we talked, laughed, and ate copious amounts of food. Marco was relaxed too. It was like he'd taken off his suit and tie and become a son, brother, and uncle.

Inside my chest, my heart warmed.

By dessert, I knew with certainty I liked Marco.

I should ask him for sex. God knows I wanted to have sex with him. A slow smile formed on my lips. Marco leaned over and kissed my cheek like it was the most natural thing in the world for him to do, then returned to his conversation with his brothers. Rachael grinned and tipped her champagne glass my way as though she approved of me, of our relationship.

But she didn't know what this was.

It would never be what they had here.

Marco and I would never have children. Never

share dinners like this with a family. We'd never have love.

No, I wouldn't ask Marco for sex because if my growing feelings for him were any sign, then I might be in jeopardy of falling in love with him.

And he didn't want love from me.

All he wanted was a woman to parade around as his wife for his job. I'd do well to remember that.

\*\*\*\*

"Thanks for dinner," I said as he pulled the Camaro to a stop in front of the Burberry mansion.

"You were quiet on the drive home."

"Was I?" I brushed my fingers through my hair which I'd left down for him. The enormous diamond on the engagement ring tangled in my hair.

"Hold still," he said, gently extracting my hair from around the ring.

With each caress of his finger, tiny shivers danced across my skin. He freed my hand and cupped it between both of his. Fire and heat flickered through my veins, but it was more than arousal for Marco as a man now, there was the pitter-patter of my heart inside my chest.

"Kennedy?"

"Hmm?"

Our gazes locked.

His tongue darted out and licked his lips.

"Thanks for tonight. You were perfect."

I said nothing. I couldn't.

His gaze dropped to my lips. "You're beautiful too." Then his gaze traveled back up to my eyes. "My family adored you."

"Your family is lovely," I said softly and drew my hand out from between his. "I should go."

I needed to go before I asked him to kiss me. To take me back to his apartment and make love to me. I almost scoffed aloud. As if we'd make love. We didn't even love each other. The well-timed reminder had me swinging open the car door and escaping to the front door of the mansion. Marco followed, watched while I keyed in the code, opened the door, and slipped inside, without him.

All I'd wanted was for Marco to take me in his arms and kiss me good night like a real fiancée.

## Chapter Thirteen

The next Wednesday I didn't text Marco as I had the last two weeks. Instead, I told Prue I was going to his apartment but left for the movies by myself. I needed distance from my growing feelings. And Marco, because if he told me to ask him one more time, I would.

I might even crawl on my knees for him.

Stranger things had happened.

Like falling for a man who'd blackmailed me.

My cell lit up with a message inside the dark theater. Marco's name flashed across the screen and a pathetic satisfaction filled me, he was the one contacting me.

Marco: **Where are you?**

Me: **Out.**

Marco: **Where?**

I contemplated not telling him. The little dots flashed on the screen waiting for me to type.

Me: **Movies.**

Marco: **With whom?**

Came his immediate response. I rolled my eyes.

Me: **Myself.**

Marco: **Which cinema?**

Me: **Doesn't matter.**

Marco: **It matters.**

Ugh, he was frustrating. How was I meant to watch a movie when he wouldn't stop texting me?

Me: **I'm trying to watch a movie.**

Marco: **Where?**

Me: **Palisade's Cinema.**

Marco: **Which movie?**

Me: **Shark Attack 3.0.**

The dots disappeared. I settled back in the seat, gobbled the popcorn, and let the movie take me away from my worries. Scary sharks in the ocean did that with ease.

A warm hand slid onto my shoulder at the same moment that a great white shark attacked the girl on the screen. I screamed and jumped, spilling the popcorn all over myself.

Beside me, a deep husky laugh sounded.

"Marco?"

He plucked popcorn from my top and ate it.

"What are you doing here?" I hissed quieter now.

"Watching a movie," he whispered and picked more popcorn from my lap this time.

His fingers grazed my crotch by accident, or maybe not, but either way, my lower region quivered into instant arousal. He continued picking up the popcorn, swiping his fingers over my body too. I grabbed his wrist.

"What are you doing?" I whisper asked.

"Eating your popcorn," he whispered. Leaning in closer to my ear he said, "I'd rather eat your pussy, but here we are."

He pried my fingers off his arm and continued eating popcorn from my lap and chest. All I could think about was him going down on me, right here, right now. I slammed my eyes shut, not even bothering to pretend to watch the movie, how could I when I was turned on?

Damp fingers drifted up the inside of my skirt. I slammed my legs together.

"Open for me," he whispered in my ear.

I shook my head.

His fingers massaged my thigh. Arousal beat a steady tempo in my heart and head, and lower in my clit and deep inside. What would it be like to have his fingers on my eager flesh? I opened my eyes and eased my legs open a fraction.

"Good girl," he whispered, sliding his fingers to my now open inner thigh. "You were such a bad girl not coming to my apartment tonight that I wanted to punish you." His fingers touched my panties and caressed the satiny material.

My legs shook with the building arousal he'd sparked in me with ease.

"You're going to sit here and let me slide my finger inside these damp panties like the dirty girl you are, and then you're going to come nice and quietly like a good girl." He traced the edge of my panties. "Yes?"

I squeezed my lips together but nodded my head. His finger slid under my panties and found the building moisture with ease. One swipe through my folds and my hips jerked on the seat.

"Stay still," he whispered. "Or would you prefer everyone to watch you come instead of merely me?"

I scanned the packed cinema and shook my head. I enjoyed watching other people but having them watch me wasn't something I'd considered I'd enjoy. He slid two fingers over my folds then up to my clit. He circled the tight bundle of nerves with the moisture he'd gathered in a slow, gentle rhythm. Gradually the pressure built until little gasps left my mouth. He placed his other hand over my mouth.

Oh, God, that made me even hotter and more desperate to come. His fingers dipped lower sparking the nerve endings around my opening until I would have begged him to fuck me if he hadn't covered my mouth with his hand. Up and down, round and round, he worked my clit and opening until there was only Marco and his fingers in my world. The orgasm rippled from my insides to start with, then exploded from my clit in wave after wave of pleasure. His fingers coaxed every last spasm from my release.

I sagged back in the seat spent and a pile of liquid mush. The lights on the stairs flickered on. The movie credits rolled, and people walked down the stairs. Marco slid his hand from my mouth but kept his other hand under my skirt.

"Sit still," he whispered.

My heart raced, we were about to get caught, but only a single man gawked our way and gave us a thumbs-up. Heat scorched a trail across my face. As the last person left, I urged Marco to take his hand out of my pants.

He laughed. "I thought you might let me keep them there all night."

I stood and squeezed in front of him. He tugged me down onto his lap and against his hard cock.

"We're not having sex in a cinema," I hissed.

"Not tonight," he said.

"Not any night. You get our wedding night and that's it." I shoved off his lap and scrambled to my feet.

He stood with me. "That's it?"

"That was part of the negotiations, remember?"

"The sex part was open to more, remember?" he threw back at me.

"Yeah, well, I don't want more than one night."

He snorted. "Stop lying to yourself and me. I don't like liars, remember that." He scowled. "I'll drive you home."

"You don't have to drive me home. I came here by myself, I sure as hell can find my way home."

"Don't I?" He raised an eyebrow. "Sorry if I think I should drive home the woman who came all over my hand."

I crossed my arms. "I didn't ask you to do that."

"No, you won't ask me for anything you want, will you?"

"Why would I when you've made it clear what this marriage is all about?" I stomped down the stairs.

"Kennedy." He caught up with me and grabbed my elbow. "What does that mean?"

"Not a damn thing," I said, as we walked down the rest of the stairs and out of the cinema. "You know what." I turned in his grip. "If you're smart, you'll figure it out."

He scowled, and we left the cinema in silence. Climbed into his car in silence. He drove to the Burberry mansion in silence. I hated every single second of it.

## Chapter Fourteen

Prue knocked on my bedroom door as I sat on the floor packing my belongings.

"I still can't believe you're moving out." She pouted.

"Me either." I shoved a book into the box.

"And getting married to Marco." She leaned against the doorjamb and crossed her ankles. "He's a good guy, I'm glad you're getting a good one. You deserve it."

I forced a smile and picked up another book.

"Kennedy, is everything all right?"

"Sure, why wouldn't it be?"

"You seem a bit off the last few days since you saw Marco on Wednesday. Did he upset you? If he did, he should buy you flowers."

"No, he doesn't need to buy me flowers. I guess I'm sad about leaving here. You guys have been my family the last three years."

"We'll always be your family." She walked into the room and passed me a book off the shelf.

I placed the paperback in the box and shut the lid.

Prue picked up my locked box from the top shelf and peered down at me. "What's in here?"

"Nothing." I stood in a hurry and tried to take the box from her.

She yanked it back and shook the box. A buzzing noise exploded from inside. Prue laughed and handed me the box.

"You won't need a vibrator now you have Marco. If he's anything like Will, he'll keep you so satisfied you'll wonder what you did for orgasms before him."

I unlocked the box and turned off the vibrator Prue inadvertently turned on when she'd shaken the box.

I may need the toy more when we were married than I had in the three years of celibacy if I stuck to the sex-only-on-our-wedding-night. What did the man expect? I'd have sex with him all the time and never develop feelings? Not that we'd even enjoyed sex yet, and I'd already developed feelings. I shut the lid on my box of well-used toys. Little did Prue know I'd used them a few times after listening or watching her and William have sex.

"I know Saturdays are your day off, but we're taking the boys to the zoo and thought you might like to come." Prue played with the long strands of her dark hair.

I grimaced remembering the ninja goat kicking my leg then my face heated recalling how Marco had given me my first non-solo orgasm in years.

"I have more to pack," I said. I waved my hand at the bookcase, but the shelves were almost empty. I only had my clothes left to pack.

Prue laughed. "Come on, the boys will love having you there too."

I scanned the room that'd been my home for three years. If I stayed here alone today, I might end up crying.

"Okay."

"Excellent. Marco is coming too. It'll be like a double date."

"What?"

"Oh, did I forget to mention Marco was coming?" She backed up to the door. "He'll be here in ten minutes and then we're leaving. Is that enough time for you to get ready?"

"I guess it'll have to be," I muttered, dusting off my backside. Did I have time to change clothes? Or do makeup? At least brush my hair which I'd piled on top of my head in a messy bun.

The doorbell peeled through the mansion.

"Oops," Prue said, "sounds like he's here already. Shall I send him up?"

"No," I snapped. "I mean, I'll be down in a minute, there's no use him coming up here."

"Sure, we'll wait until you're ready," Prue said then disappeared out of my room shutting the door behind her.

For crying out loud, could I catch a break from any of this? I tossed the locked box into the packing box and shut the lid, sealing it with tape. I doubt I'd need my toys over the next week, and even if I did, I'd end up imagining the vibrator was Marco and I didn't need that. Seeing him today would be bad enough.

I wrenched open a drawer, changed my t-shirt to a pretty flowery sleeveless shirt that tied at my waist. Leaving on the shorts, I shoved my feet into a pair of sneakers, then I dashed into the bathroom, flicked powder over my face, and ran a coat of pale-pink lip gloss over my lips. That'd have to do.

Everyone's voices drifted from the foyer. The twins sounded excited. I was doing this for them. I squared my shoulders and made my way down the stairs. Marco glanced up the moment I walked into view. The second he saw me, he smiled, then a dark expression passed over his face, and frown lines appeared between his eyes. Guess he was still annoyed about me going to the movies Wednesday night. Well, tough luck. I didn't owe him any days of the week.

"Hi," I said, hesitating at the bottom of the stairs. "I'm ready, let's go."

Prue and William stared at me like I was crazy. Marco crossed the small distance, slid his hands to my waist, leaned forward, and touched his lips to my cheek.

"Hello, my beautiful fiancée."

If it was real, I might have swooned against his firm chest. I caught sight of Prue's questioning stare. I placed my hands around his neck and stepped into his hold.

"I missed you," I said.

His eyebrows shot up, but behind him, Prue's face smoothed out.

"Don't worry, sweetheart, we'll be together soon." His thumbs stroked the tight muscles in my lower back.

"One more week. Everything is ready, except you haven't told me who you've picked for your two groomsmen."

Marco nodded at William. "William for my best man of course, which works out well since Prue is your matron of honor."

"Matron of honor sounds frightful, like I'm a nun or something," Prue said.

"Don't worry, Prue," William said. "I'll dishonor you in every way I can throughout the night."

Prue flung her arms around William's waist and kissed him.

I cleared my throat. "Who else did you pick? We need another groomsman since my sister is a bridesmaid."

"My friend Callan. You haven't met him yet."

I'd met none of Marco's friends yet. He'd met none of mine from back home, but he was already friends with Prue and Tiff.

"We've organized your buck's night for next Friday," William said.

"Shit," Prue said, "I'm a bad matron of honor, I haven't organized a hen's night for you."

"You don't need to…"

"Hell, yeah, I do. Male strippers, booze, oh crap, I

can't drink. But you can. I'll get you so drunk you won't be able to walk down the aisle the next day."

"Prue, that's not a good idea," Marco said. "She's wearing her grandmother's vintage wedding gown."

"I suppose we can't have her throwing up on the dress."

"Mom, can we go now?" Tuck tugged on Prue's hand.

"Sure can, buddy. Uncle Gabe will have the car ready for us out the back." Prue turned to us. "We'll see you at the zoo."

Marco took my hand in his and led me out the front door to his Camaro. We drove to the zoo in silence. This was getting ridiculous. Were we going to get married without speaking to each other?

"We can't go the entire day without talking," I said.

"We spoke back at the mansion."

He parked the car and we made our way to the zoo entrance. Since he drove like a maniac, we were there before the others. I stepped under the shade of a tree since the sun was shining with a sweltering glare. Marco followed me. He looked good dressed in a pair of designer jeans and navy shirt. Dark sunglasses hid his eyes and gave him the elusive rich man vibe.

This couldn't go on for the rest of the day. Not in front of Prue and William and the twins. This was supposed to be a fun day at the zoo.

"I'm sorry if I upset you by going to the movies last night."

He shoved his hands in his pockets.

"I didn't realize the Wednesday night thing was a compulsory event."

"It wasn't, and it isn't."

"This will take a bit of getting used to for both of

us."

"It'll be easier when we're married and living together."

*Will it?* I wanted to ask but bit the inside of my cheek instead. The metallic taste of blood mingled with my saliva. Prue, William, and the twins arrived, and we walked into the zoo together led by the boys' enthusiasm.

Marco held my hand once more and played the perfect doting fiancé in front of his friends. The kids pointed out the animals at each enclosure with excited waving of their hands. Sometimes the boys walked with us, one of them holding our hands and forcing us apart, then they'd switch and do the same thing to their mom and dad. It amused me how they wanted to be the center of attention all the time. We stopped for lunch in the cafeteria and watched the keepers talk about the pelicans, then headed to my most dreaded place—the petting zoo.

"What's wrong?" Marco asked after we walked through the gate.

"Ninja goats."

He laughed. "Here they come with their swords."

"Get ready to run," I said in all earnestness.

He laughed harder, then harder still when the goats ventured closer to us, and I ducked behind his back.

"Come on, Kennedy, they don't seem vicious at all."

"You wait," I said, "as soon as you finish feeding them, they'll turn on you."

"I'm scared," he drawled. He gave them another handful of pellets from his pouch and patted one on the back. "Their fur is wiry. Touch it."

"No, thanks. I'm safe behind you and that's where I'm staying until we leave."

He tipped the last of the pellets into his hand. "At

least you're happy to use me for something."

The goats gobbled the remaining pellets then sniffed Marco's hands, the empty bag, and his pockets. When they'd finished inspecting him, they butted heads with each other, turned, and kicked. Marco's sunglasses flew from his face as his head snapped to the side.

"What the f … flipping … ah goat?" he growled, glancing around at all the young children in the petting zoo.

"I told you." I stayed right where I was until the goats walked on to the next group of people offering pellets.

Marco bent and picked up his sunglasses, his firm butt pressing into me since I hadn't budged. He peered at me over his shoulder, placed the bent sunglasses back on his face, and stood.

Prue trotted over laughing. "Oh my God, that was hilarious. I wish I'd had the video camera on you then, Marco."

"The goat got you square in the face," William said.

"What?" I tugged Marco's sunglasses from his face.

A bruise was already forming between his brows.

"Let's get you home and put ice on your face."

"I'm fine." He scowled.

I put the sunglasses back on his face and squatted in front of the kids. "Boys, Uncle Marco and I are going home now."

"Bye," they said in unison and threw their arms around my neck.

Marco ruffled their hair and high-fived them.

"Come on, my big protector." I wrapped an arm around his waist and guided him out of the zoo.

We stopped at his car.

"How's your head feeling?"

"It's sore now." He touched a hand to his forehead and grimaced.

"Should I drive?"

"Do you know how to drive a stick?"

I rolled my eyes. "Yes."

He handed me the keys and sat in the passenger seat letting out a deep sigh. Well, that was easier than I thought it was going to be.

"I'm going to hear I told you so for the rest of our lives, aren't I?"

"For sure." I grinned. "Ninja goats are a real thing."

"Bastards is what they are."

I started the Camaro, set the navigation system, and drove to his apartment at a much slower speed than he would have driven. It took me longer than Marco to get through the heavy traffic, but we arrived at his apartment building and he told me to park in the underground garage. We took the lift straight up to his penthouse apartment. I urged him into the kitchen, got ice out of the freezer, wrapped the cubes in a cloth, and lifted the homemade ice pack to his forehead.

A smirk stretched my lips.

"Pretty smug, aren't you?"

"Yep."

"Who is going to believe a goat kicked me in the face?"

I snickered. "Not many people. Let's hope there's no bruise for the wedding photos, otherwise you'll be telling everyone anytime they see them."

"The humiliation keeps rolling on in."

I laughed. "Poor Marco, want me to kiss it better?"

"Yeah, I do."

I eased the ice away from his forehead, stood on my tippy-toes, and with the barest of touches I kissed my lips to the mark.

"There, all better." I replaced the ice.

"My nose is sore too."

"Probably from the sunglasses. I wonder if you'll get black eyes too?" I kissed the bridge of his nose.

"Let's hope not." He circled my wrist holding the ice and shifted it a fraction lower over the bridge of his nose. "Last time I got a black eye was when I was in college."

"I bet you were hot back then too."

His lips twitched. I dropped my gaze to the motion.

"I bet you were hot in your college days too," he said in that husky tone that did things to my insides.

"A total blonde babe," I said.

"You still are." He let go of my wrist to tug on the band holding my messy bun in place.

My hair fell free over my shoulders. He combed through the tangled tresses with his fingers, sending tiny shivers through my skull.

"That's better. I'm looking forward to seeing all this blonde hair spread out on my sheets." He cupped the back of my head and lowered his lips to mine.

Neither of us froze this time. The kiss was slow, lips against lips, shaping and tasting, building with every minute, first a tiny flicker of his tongue against the seam of my lips, then a sure swipe. I opened my mouth and let him inside. He kept his tongue as slow as his lips until he drugged me to everything but his mouth and tongue on mine.

A moan built in my throat and tumbled free. His other hand slid up my back, pressed between my shoulder blades, and drew me closer until our chests touched. My already hard nipples rejoiced at the contact. Then his lips trailed to the edge of my mouth, along my jaw, and down my neck. I dropped the ice bag with a loud splat on the floor.

The noise brought me to my senses. I shoved my hands against his chest, and he released me straightaway.

"What was that?" I touched my lips with shaking fingers.

"A kiss." He bent and picked up the ice before the cubes melted all over the floor.

"Why?"

"Because I wanted to." He held the ice to his forehead himself this time. "You wanted to kiss me too, otherwise you wouldn't have let me or kissed me back."

"I can't … we can't…"

I couldn't kiss him, not when I'd developed feelings for him. Not when he didn't want my feelings.

"Right." He let out a loud breath. "Not until our wedding night." His face paled, and he swayed.

"Quick." I rushed back to his side. "Sit down."

"I'm okay. I simply need painkillers. My head is thumping."

"Where are they?"

"In my en suite"

*Of course they were.*

I wrapped an arm around his waist and walked with him to his bedroom, sat him on the bed, and stepped into the bathroom in search of the painkillers. The first thing I found was a drawer full of condoms. At least it was good to know he practiced safe sex. I shoved the drawer closed and checked the next one. Bingo. I walked back out waving the packet, but he'd stripped his shirt and laid back on the pillows with his eyes closed. I took a minute running my gaze over his chest. What would it be like to touch our naked chests together?

"You got the pills?" Marco asked.

I jumped, caught checking him out. "Yes." I took the few steps to the bed and handed him the packet. "You don't think you've got a concussion, do you?"

"No. I've had one of those too, this is nothing like a concussion."

"That's good."

He popped the pills in his mouth and drank from the water bottle beside his bed.

"But you should stay just in case."

"Stay here? With you?" I swallowed.

"Why not? You'll be staying with me all the time after next week."

"True," I said. *What harm would one night do?*

He patted the bed. I toed off my shoes and climbed onto the mattress.

"Do you want the television on?"

"What television?"

"Hit the button on top of the headboard."

I spun around and tapped the button. A television slid down from the ceiling at the foot of the bed.

"So cool. How do I change the channels?"

"Say what channel you want, and it'll come on."

"Um, adults' channel."

Marco laughed.

"It was the only one I could think of. Unless you wanted to watch kids' shows?"

"That's okay, Kennedy, I'm happy to watch porn with you anytime you want."

I slid under the sheets, they were as silky as the ones in the Burberry mansion. Marco unbuttoned his slacks, slid them down his legs until he was in his black boxer shorts, and joined me under the sheets as sounds of people having sex rang from the television screen. I tugged a pillow from behind my back and hugged the downy comfort to my chest.

"Don't worry, you've made it clear you don't want me."

It wasn't that I didn't want him. It was *because* I wanted him. All of him. His body and his heart.

"I won't kiss you or touch you except on our wedding night."

That was what I wanted, wasn't it?

\*\*\*\*

Shit. I sat up with a start. I hadn't meant to fall asleep in Marco's bed, but it'd been too comfortable. To my surprise, the sounds of sex put me to sleep instead of making me hot and bothered like usual. But Marco's kiss was in my mind. His touch seared its presence into my flesh.

My body didn't want anyone or anything but him.

He rolled over and opened his eyes. "You're here."

"Yeah." I lightly ran my finger over his forehead. "No lump. That's good and only a little red mark. You must have a tough head." My fingers trailed up into his hair.

His eyes took on a deep glow before they drifted shut.

Emotions clamored around my heart. I stroked my fingers through the thick mass of his hair again and again until Marco drifted back to sleep. After a long time of touching him for the pleasure of it, I slid out of bed and did the walk of shame in my creased slept-in clothes, through the lobby and into the Uber. I didn't leave a note or anything. He knew where I was if he wanted to find me.

Prue gave me two thumbs-up when I walked through the door of the mansion. I disappeared upstairs and into my room without saying a word. Let her think whatever she wanted. It was better for everyone if they thought I was having sex with Marco, if they believed we were marrying for the right reasons.

The reasons were all muddled in my head now. What was the right reason? What was the wrong reason? Would we be able to make the marriage work no matter what the reason?

## Chapter Fifteen

Marco sent a text message at seven in the morning on Wednesday.

Marco: **My apartment. Seven o'clock tonight. Be there.**

I didn't respond, but we both knew I'd go. The tone in the message came across as if he were angry. Or even displeased. That made me smile. Served him right all his stupid negotiations didn't consider human emotions. *My emotions.*

The day dragged by as my gaze wandered back to the time over and over again while looking after the twins. We played toy cars, swam in the pool, played in the park, and ate dinner with Prue and William. I even checked the clock during dinner which made Prue smile and shoo me off to get ready the second I'd scraped the last forkful of risotto into my mouth.

I put on a pastel-pink dress hanging to my knees that made me look pretty and young. Another suit of armor against Marco. Which used to work against other men, but I doubted looking younger would work against Marco now he knew what I hid under the camouflage of sweet and innocent. The Uber delivered me to his apartment building at five minutes to seven. The concierge greeted me with a cheerful smile and waved me on up, making me seem important, as if I belonged in this extravagant world.

I half expected Marco to be waiting at the door holding a clock in his hand, but he wasn't. I knocked on the door with one minute to spare. He made me wait the entire minute before opening the door. He wore an immaculate black suit and gray tie matching his eyes. My heart did this little irregular beat, then pounded inside my chest.

"Follow me," he said.

"Um, hello to you too," I said, chasing after him down the hallway.

He stopped outside the bedroom he'd set the cameras in. My mouth turned dry.

"Hello, Kennedy," he said in that husky tone that sent a shiver down my spine.

"Why are we here?" I nodded at the closed door and what lay behind it.

"You've taken things too far this time." He pinned me with his deep gray eyes. "We fell asleep together. I expected to wake up together. You couldn't even give me the courtesy of saying good-bye, could you?"

I swallowed and opened my mouth. But he was right, it was a shitty thing to do, leaving the way I did. Like we weren't engaged and about to be married. Like spending the night sleeping in the same bed meant nothing to me. That was the problem, the night meant more than it should.

He turned the handle and pushed the door open. "After you."

"I'm not having sex with you," I said, walking into the room anyway.

"I didn't say you were. Tonight." He closed the door, walked around to all the cameras, and switched them on. "Sit on the bed and take your punishment."

*Punishment?* The last time he'd punished me, he'd given me an orgasm in the movie theatre. I perched on the end of the bed and crossed my legs at the ankles as desire swamped my body.

"Look at you pretending to be all sweet and proper when we both know you're a dirty, dirty girl." He sat beside me, leaving an inch between our thighs.

I flicked my eyes from one camera to the next.

What would this look like on video? Him in his suit and tie, me in my pretty dress.

"Lower your dress, Kennedy, show the camera how dirty you are."

"What?" I snapped my head up to meet his eyes.

"You heard me, now do it." He unbuttoned his pants and slid down the zip.

"Um." My mouth went dry. Whatever this was I liked it. I liked the way he was talking to me. Directing me. Giving me his orders.

Tiny shivers danced over my skin as I tugged one spaghetti strap then the other off my shoulders. The top of the dress slid to my waist and left my lace-covered breasts exposed.

"Your nipples are begging for my mouth." He eased his erection from his boxer shorts and slid his hand down the length. "Would you like me to suck them?"

"I…" I couldn't take my eyes off his hand working along his hard cock. He was so thick and long that I had to squeeze my legs together.

"Answer me."

"Yes," I snapped.

"Good girl," he said in that deep husky tone. "Now on your knees."

The way he said "good girl" had me sliding to the floor on my knees in front of him. His hand worked his straining length. My mouth watered to lean forward and take him in my mouth. To learn every vein and pulse of need with my tongue and lips. Most of all to taste him, make him mine. I leaned forward.

"No, stay there," he snapped.

I sat back with a loud humph and disgruntled pout.

My response thrust him over the edge into release. He groaned a deep growl making my insides wish he'd make the noise while buried deep inside me. His cock pulsed and spurted his release up over his suit jacket and high enough to get his tie. He gave himself one last squeeze eking out the remaining drops of cum.

"Dirty girl, look what you made me do." He tucked his cock back into his pants and zipped himself up. "Take off my jacket and tie and go clean them up."

I glared up at him. Did he expect me to undress him and clean up his mess?

He cupped my face and tilted up my chin. We stared at each other for the longest time until a sense of peace washed over me. Being on my knees doing what he said filled me with an emotion I'd never experienced before, it wasn't love, but more. A man who knew what I needed, and in all honesty, I needed this asshole side of him. I undid his jacket buttons, stood, and eased the fabric from his shoulders. I untied his tie next and slid the silk from his thick throat.

"Good girl," he said. He stood and lifted my straps back up my arms and covered my breasts. He kissed the top of my head and switched off all the video cameras effectively dismissing me.

The part of me that loved being treated like this glowed at being recognized because Marco accepted this side of me. A side I'd kept hidden and shown no one else.

I left and carried his clothes to the laundry room, the scent of his cum was heady and erotic, that if he'd come on his naked body, I'd want to lick him clean. Even more, if he told me to. Why did I get turned on when he acted like an asshole to me? I scrubbed his clothes clean in the sink then hung them up to dry. They'd still need dry cleaning but at least they wouldn't stain now.

When I left the room I found Marco sitting on the lounge looking mighty relaxed with a glass of wine and heavy metal music blaring through the speakers.

"Thanks for coming," he said. "I'll see you Saturday down the end of the aisle."

"What?" I gasped. That was it? He'd asked me to come over and watch him masturbate. And I get nothing?

"Enjoy your hen's night." He sipped his wine. "I'll enjoy my buck's night."

"No doubt you will." I folded my arms over my chest. *Did he use me?*

"Lots of strippers." He grinned.

"You're an ass."

"I'll see lots of those too."

"Could you be any more infuriating?" I tapped my foot for good measure.

"You know what's infuriating?" He stood and got in my face. "You."

"Me?" I poked a finger into his chest. "It's you."

He caught my finger in his hand. "All you had to do was ask, but no, you couldn't, could you?"

"I am not asking you for sex," I ground out through my teeth.

"Would it be so bad? Are you repulsed by me?"

"If I was, I wouldn't have let you give me two orgasms or watch you give yourself one."

"What, then?" He released my finger.

I shook my head. I couldn't tell him I wanted more than a marriage of convenience. I wanted him to have feelings for me too. The same feelings I had for him.

"Give me something," he lowered his voice.

"I can't."

"Go." He stepped back. "Before I don't let you go, and I go back on my word, throw you on the sofa, and screw you until you can't move *before we're married*." He hissed the last words.

I hurried to the door and ducked into the hallway, my heart hammering inside my chest because I didn't want him to let me go. Come Saturday he wouldn't. I'd be his in every way possible. Would I be able to hide my feelings from Marco after we had sex?

## Chapter Sixteen

"Woo-hoo!" Prue screamed at the top of her lungs in the limousine on the way to my hen's night. "A girl's night out. I can't believe I didn't think of doing this for my wedding renewal."

"Me either," Tiff said. "Strippers, drinks, fun. I didn't have a hen's night either."

"You can both celebrate with me," I said, sipping on the glass of champagne.

"We intend to," Prue said.

My sister, six cousins, Mom, and two aunts were with us too, having already arrived in Los Angeles for the wedding tomorrow. My family was staying at Prue's Resort and Day Spa too.

Prue booked out the entire famous strip joint, Man-O-Hunk. Gabe drove the limousine as he always drove the Burberrys around, but I had a feeling William sent Gabe along to monitor us. I felt bad for the guy having to take his daughter Tiffany to a male strip joint, but he was one of the coolest dads I'd ever met.

I shuddered to think how my dad and brother were getting along with Marco at his buck's night. No doubt Dad would give him more disapproving looks. But Marco was a grown man and could take care of himself. If they got in a fight, then that was their problem.

Not mine.

Nope.

I'd hang onto that as long as possible.

Gabe pulled the limousine to a stop in front of the flashing neon lights of the strip joint and opened the door. We all piled out of the car and made our way inside. More neon lights flashed above the bar. An almost naked man escorted us up to our table, took our drink orders, and strutted away to the wolf whistles of my cousins. My aunts shook their heads but grinned.

Once the waiter returned with our drinks, the lights dimmed and the music changed. A man in a firefighter's outfit strutted onto the stage gyrating his hips to the beats of the song. He ripped open his top displaying washboard abs. More hooting from my relatives. His hands landed on the waist of his pants, and he ripped them off with an exaggerated roll of his hips, his thong-covered dick flopped about in front of my face.

My cheeks heated, and I turned my face to the side.

Prue bumped shoulders with me. "Loosen up, girl. It's a bit of fun."

The stripper stepped away from me. It sucked having the bride-to-be sash over my shoulder and chest. The strippers would target me all night. I'd have to slip the sash onto someone else later in the night. Maybe Prue, she'd enjoy the attention.

The firefighter left and a police officer took center stage twirling a set of handcuffs. He extended his hand to me and dragged me onto the stage with helpful shoving from my friends and family. The police officer slapped the handcuffs on my wrists and sat me on a chair. He gave me a lap dance in front of everyone, rubbing his ass and junk on my lap and then in my face.

Yet all I wanted was for the man to be Marco shoving his cock in my face.

When the song was over, I scampered from the stage and downed my drink. The semi-naked waiter placed another cocktail in front of me.

Prue laughed. "You should have seen your face. I took a photo and sent it to Will."

"You did not." I gasped. No, that wouldn't be good. William would show Marco. But would it upset Marco? Or wouldn't he care? Or would he be getting his own stripper's ass and breasts in his face? And loving every minute.

As I'd expected, Prue showed me a photo William sent her of Marco and a stripper sitting on his lap. Unexpected tears burned the backs of my eyes. I hurried from the table and disappeared into the bathroom.

Zara followed me. "Hey." She leaned against the sink beside me where I was splashing my face with water.

"Don't," I said, my voice catching at the end.

"I won't, but I'm here if you need to talk."

I turned off the tap and watched the last of the water drip down the drain. "I've fallen for Marco."

"That's a good thing since you're marrying him."

"You'd think." I opened my handbag and started fixing my makeup.

"You're scared he doesn't feel the same way," she said in her way-too-perceptive way.

"I know he doesn't."

"Babe, any man who is marrying you would be a fool to not fall for you, and Marco doesn't come across as a fool. He's smart, determined, and old enough to know how to treat you right."

"You figured all that after meeting him once?"

"I can pinpoint anyone's character after ten minutes. It's a skill." She brushed her knuckles on her chest, then blew on them.

I ran the eyeliner under my eyes. "When are you getting a job?"

"I've applied for some here in Los Angeles."

"You have?" I squealed. "I'll have my sister in the same state!"

"Fingers crossed." She held up her crossed fingers. "I'll need somewhere to crash if I do get the job."

"Wait, I have the perfect solution." I grabbed her hand, dragged her out of the bathroom, and back to the table. "Prue, I found your night nanny."

Prue glanced up at us.

"Me?" Zara asked. "I don't know."

"It's perfect," I said. "The boys sleep through the night and Prue or William will do the night feeds anyway when she gives birth. Won't you, Prue?"

"I do, or Will fetches me the baby."

"So you're only there in case one twin wakes up. You could handle putting one sleepy toddler back to bed."

Prue tilted her head. "It wouldn't be much work, but you could have Kennedy's room."

"Okay, I'll do it until I get a psychologist job and find a place," Zara said. "Then you'll have to find someone else."

"Deal." Prue held out her hand. "This is good. Thank you, Kennedy."

"It's the least I could do." I sunk into a chair and turned my attention to the stage.

Another stripper danced decorated in strange body paint and tribal music playing to his moves. I tapped my foot in time. Zara was always right about people. She possessed a genuine gift. A thrill zoomed through my veins, the possibility of Marco falling for me more real than I dared to hope.

**\*\*\*\***

"Ugh," Zara said, buttoning up my wedding dress. "Why did I drink so much?"

I laughed. "Glad I didn't."

"You look like the radiant bride. How much did you drink?"

"Four cocktails."

"I should have stopped at four. These buttons are

stupid, how are you meant to get them off tonight?"

"That'll be my husband's job."

"He's going to love you in this dress," Prue said.

*Love.* There was that word that Marco said wouldn't happen. It was too late for me to not love him.

"Last one," Zara said. "There. Good luck to Marco getting them undone later."

"It'll be like opening a present wrapped in tape." Prue giggled.

"Let's go," I said, picking up my bouquet of peonies that cost a small fortune.

"Someone's eager." Prue picked up her posy and handed Zara hers. "Can't blame you, though, wedding night sex is amazing. The first time Will and I had sex I still had those shoes on."

"These shoes I'm wearing?" I gasped.

"Yes." She smirked. "Enjoy."

"You're evil."

"In a good way."

Zara laughed. "A healthy sex life is the best thing for a marriage."

"No psychobabble today, please."

"Did you tell Mom that too?"

I lifted my eyes to the ceiling. "Are her and Dad still against this marriage?"

"Oh, you should have heard them the last few weeks."

"Um, no, thanks."

"Your parents aren't happy for you?" Prue frowned.

"Not really. I guess it was a surprise we were getting married so soon."

"I was a little surprised too. Marco has a huge hang-up with his ex-girlfriend and how she cheated on him, got pregnant, and tried to convince him the baby was his. Will said he didn't do relationships after her. You two have known each other for years. I never would have suspected anything between you two. You were always polite to each other."

"I guess we've grown on each other." I shrugged for what else could I tell Prue? Marco blackmailed me into marrying him, otherwise he'd tell Prue and William I watched them have sex.

"Sound basis for a marriage, then," Zara said, eyeing me with a hint of doubt in her eyes.

"Absolutely." I nodded. "Let's go."

Zara opened the door without another word. Prue led the way through the resort to where Dad waited in front of the massive glass doors leading to the beach and where the guests sat along the red carpet aisle.

"You're very handsome, Daddy." I kissed his cheek.

"You are stunning." He tucked my hand through his arm. "Are you sure about this? We can always turn around and take you back home."

I squeezed his arm. "I'm sure."

He squeezed my arm back. "I thought I'd give you the last chance."

I smiled up at my dad. He'd been my protector all my life, but he hadn't been able to stop me from insisting on being with my ex-boyfriend or from me getting hurt by my ex's actions. He wouldn't stop me now even if it meant I'd get hurt again, and with the way I'd developed feelings for Marco who knew what would happen between us. Handing me off to Marco must be hard on him.

"I appreciate that, Daddy."

Attendants opened the doors and Prue and Zara walked down the aisle. Dad and I stepped into the open doorways. Marco stared down the aisle, his gaze started at my feet and drifted up to my body then to my face. Heat, passion, and possession marked his handsome face. Every nerve ending in my body flared to life like his gaze alone sent me to the peak of being desired.

Dad sighed. "When a man looks at his bride like she's the best thing he's ever seen, then that's all the proof I need you'll be happy."

"Thanks, Daddy," I whispered.

The song I'd chosen to walk down the aisle trickled from the speakers. "Marry You" by Bruno Mars. Marco laughed but crooked his finger at me. Dad walked me down the aisle, shook Marco's hand, and handed me over like I was a piece of property being sold.

"I'm looking for something dumb to do," I said.

"I don't doubt it." He walked us up to the celebrant. "You are breathtaking."

"Thank you," I said as he took my hands in his and faced me.

"This is by far the least dumb thing I've ever done." He stroked his thumbs over my wrists.

My heart raced so fast my pulse pounded in my head and drowned out the words from the celebrant. I repeated the words at the right time, though, and Marco slid a wedding band onto my finger. He did the same, and I placed a wedding ring on his finger. A sense of satisfaction surged through me—he was mine and everyone in the world would see my ring on his finger.

"You may now kiss the bride," the celebrant said.

Marco tugged me closer, trapping our hands together between our chests, then kissed me as he'd never kissed me before. His lips stirred against mine and I was powerless to stop my lips from answering his. They danced together as though we were now joined body and soul.

Applause broke out. We parted and made our way

down the aisle to our family and friends' congratulations.

This fake wedding had the potential to be the best day of my life.

\*\*\*\*

The wedding reception was a blast. Everyone was happy and full of enthusiasm for us. They filled my heart with even more love. Marco's bosses had even come, and we'd spent some time chatting with them. Afterward, Marco told me they loved me and they'd make him a partner that week. At least he'd gotten what he'd wanted out of this marriage.

"Hey, I forgot to tell you." Callan, Marco's friend and groomsman leaned across the bridal table. "I'll have the keys to your new house on Monday."

"What house?" I asked.

"It was a surprise." Marco glared at Callan.

"Shit, sorry." Callan hung his head but smirked.

"Are you telling me you purchased us a house without me even looking at it?"

"Well, yes."

I narrowed my eyes. "Don't you think I should have at least had some say in the house?"

Marco elbowed Callan in the ribs. "Douchebag."

"Don't blame this on him." I shoved back my chair.

"Kennedy, don't make a scene." He placed his hand on my elbow and maneuvered me onto the dance floor.

"I don't want to dance with you."

"Too bad, I do." He gathered me into his arms. "Besides, you said you wanted to live near Prue and the opportunity presented itself, so I took it."

I swayed with him in time to the music as all eyes landed on us. He was right, I shouldn't make a scene at our wedding reception.

"Is it near Prue?"

"Right next door to be exact."

I squealed, threw my arms around his neck, and planted kisses all over his face.

He laughed and hauled me closer. "So you approve now?"

"Yes." I settled back into his embrace. "You should have led with that."

"That was my plan for when I picked up the keys and showed you the house, but Callan ruined my surprise."

I glanced over at Callan. He'd exchanged seats and was now sitting next to Zara chatting away. Flirting, by the looks of it.

"It looks like he had an ulterior motive." I nodded at the table.

"Poor Zara," Marco drawled.

"What? Should I go warn her to stay away from him?"

Marco laughed. "It's nothing bad. Callan is eccentric in his tastes."

"As in?"

"You'll figure it out later tonight."

"What do you mean?"

"We're staying the night at his beach house down the road from here. You'll see later."

"We're not staying here?"

"No. I intend to make you scream many times. I figured you wouldn't want your dad to come running with his gun and shoot me. Or perhaps you do?"

I quivered at his words. This was it. We would have sex tonight. For the first and last time. Yep, only time. My heart was already aching inside my chest at only having him once.

"Being alone is a good idea."

"I'm glad you agree with me for once." He dipped his head to my neck and nuzzled my skin with his mouth. "As beautiful as you are in this wedding dress, I can't wait to get you out of it, naked and crying out in pleasure."

The band switched songs and soft metal beat out a hard tune. He lifted his head and grinned.

"Is this the surprise?"

"Yes, I didn't want to frighten everyone with heavy metal. This is a suitable compromise."

He tipped my chin up with his finger. "So many layers," he said. "You keep surprising me at every turn."

I stepped back and shimmied my booty to the music. Marco laughed and joined me in dancing our wedding night away until the wee hours of the morning.

In the end, everyone urged us toward the door, otherwise we might never have left, we were having too much fun.

Marco's parents kissed my cheek, told me they'd see me soon for a family dinner. The rest of his family were as nice as his parents.

Dad shook Marco's hand. Mom even hugged him. What the hell was going on? I kissed Daddy's cheek and hugged Mom while Marco chatted with Callan.

"Come home for a visit soon, both of you." Mom patted my cheek.

"Sure," I said, even though I didn't know if Marco would go back to my family's home in Arizona after our last visit.

"I'm glad you two developed feelings for each other." Mom patted my cheek again. "It makes me feel a lot better about this marriage."

"Ready?" Marco circled my waist with his arm.

My body curved into his on its own volition, wanting to be surrounded by the warmth and protection of my husband.

Trust Mom to see I had feelings for Marco, but did I dare hope he had feelings for me too?

## Chapter Seventeen

A short drive down the coast and we arrived at Callan's spectacular beachfront mansion. Marco keyed in the password on the high-tech security system and led me inside. Glass windows made up the expanse of the walls facing the beach. In the night's darkness, the coastal lights sparkled and winked in a breathtaking display.

"Beautiful view," I said, moving closer to the window.

"We're not here for the view." Marco stood at the edge of the room and shoved his hands deep into his pants pockets.

"No, we're not." I left the view and walked over to him. "So, where are we doing this?"

His lips twitched. "Not here, that's for sure."

"Why? Don't you think we can have sex here?"

"Oh, we can have sex anywhere, but I set the camera up in the bedroom."

"Camera?"

He slid a hand from his pocket and cupped the back of my head. "I intend to watch tonight many times."

I gulped.

He tracked his hand down my arm sending a ripple of awareness along my skin and threaded his fingers with mine, then walked us down the hallway to a dark room. Marco flicked on the lights, and they lit up the bedroom. He drew the blinds over another floor-to-ceiling window and cut off the view. A massive king-size bed sat in the center of the room, at the foot of the bed sat an armchair, and beside the chair was a camera on a tripod. There was nothing out of the ordinary about the house to give me a clue about Marco's earlier comment.

"I don't understand what you meant about Callan. His house is delightful."

"Open the wardrobe." Marco tipped his head at the wall-length cupboard.

I eased a door open half expecting the bogeyman to jump out at me. When nothing scared me, I tugged open a drawer. Inside was an assortment of whips. I snapped my gaze to Marco.

He smirked.

I slammed the drawer shut and closed the door in a hurry. "I'm not … you're not … we're not…"

"Relax," Marco said. "I'm not into pain either."

My shoulders sagged.

Marco switched on the camera and sat in the chair. The atmosphere in the room changed to a heady expectation. This was it. I popped a button on my long sleeve.

"Leave it," Marco said. "I'll undress you."

My hands fell to my sides in a nervous gesture. I met his heated gaze and ran my tongue over my lips.

"Um … it's been three years."

His eyebrows rose, but he crooked his finger. I walked closer to Marco and stopped in front of the chair and camera.

"We have all night," he said. "I won't do anything to hurt you."

I nodded and wet my dry lips.

He stood with slow, controlled movements, and plucked the tiara then a pin from my updo. "I like your hair down." He extracted pin after pin until my long hair cascaded over my shoulders. Each time his fingers shifted in my hair a shiver of awareness rippled through me. By the time he finished, I was desperate for more.

"You are magnificent in this dress. I can see why you wanted to go to your parents' house and get it."

"Thank you. Sorry about my parents."

"Your dad and I got along all right at my buck's

night. We arrived at a bit of an understanding."

I narrowed my eyes. "I didn't like the stripper with her breasts in your face."

"Can't say I enjoyed seeing an almost naked man sitting on your lap."

*What did that mean? For him? For me?*

"Me either. I ended up putting my bride sash on everyone else and made sure the lap dances never danced my way again."

He cupped my face with a hand. "Full of surprises." He traced his thumb over my bottom lip. "What surprises do you have under this dress?"

"You'll have to take the gown off to find out."

His lips spread into a sensual grin. He stepped behind me leaving me facing the camera. One by one he slid the pearl buttons on the back of the dress open, his fingers skimming my flesh with each infinitesimal movement. I stared at the picture on the wall behind the camera trying to take my mind off how every brief touch of his fingers made me so needy. When he'd released all the buttons, he traced his palms up my spine to my shoulders and slid the material down my arms.

"Blue," he said, a hint of shock tinging his voice.

"Tiff made the underwear for me as my something blue."

"Something old was the dress?" He unbuttoned the pearls at my wrists.

"Yes. Something new was the tiara."

"My princess." He eased the dress sleeves from my arms with nimble fingers on the delicate material until I stood half-naked with the dress around my waist. "What was the something borrowed?"

I laughed. "You don't want to know."

He stepped in front of me and lowered the dress to my ankles, kneeling as he did so. I stepped out of the gown being careful not to stand on the old fabric. Marco caught my ankle in a firm hold.

"Are these Prue's shoes from the night we listened to them outside William's office?"

I squished my lips together and nodded.

He chuckled and removed the shoes from one foot then the other, then gathered up the wedding dress and opened the wardrobe that was a wardrobe this time and not a place for sex toys. Marco hung the gown on a hanger. My heart exploded with even more emotion for the man. Who took the time to hang a wedding dress on their wedding night? This man. My husband. He understood how much the dress meant to me.

Marco stepped behind me again, sliding his hands to my waist and up my rib cage. He cupped my breasts and teased my nipples over the top of the lacey blue fabric.

"You don't like something, tell me to stop and I will."

I nodded. So far, I loved every second his hands were on me. I leaned back into his hold, my half-naked body rubbed against his, still dressed in a tuxedo.

"Aren't you taking your clothes off? Or do you want me to do it?"

"Not yet." He slid my strapless bra down, popping my breasts free from the confines of the lace.

Cool air hit my hard nipples, then his warm hands were on them again, stroking the softness of my breasts with his knuckles.

"So soft," he murmured, skimming across my nipples from the swell of my breast to my center and back again.

Sparks of arousal shot from my breasts to my core over and over again until my stomach quivered with the need to experience his fingers lower. His hands glided lower as though he'd read my mind. My muscles bunched under his fingers. He traced the top of my boy-leg lace panties until they were damp with my arousal. At last, he brushed across the apex of my mound. A moan escaped my throat. His hand dipped inside my panties and found my wetness.

"So wet," he whispered in my ear. "Look at the camera, Kennedy. Let me watch your face as you come on my fingers."

My gaze snapped to the flashing light on the video camera. Thinking about him watching this—us—later made a fresh flood of moisture gather on his fingers. He gathered the wetness at my entrance and stroked my clit with feather-light touches, driving me insane. My inner muscles clenched with the need for more, to have him inside me. I lifted a hand to the back of his neck and rammed my butt into the thickness of his arousal. His erection rubbed between my ass cheeks. I wanted him inside me. I rose on my tippy-toes and ground down. His finger slid inside me.

"Yes," I cried out.

It'd been too long since any man touched me like this, my fingers were smaller, Marco's finger was thick and firm. He pumped one finger along my channel while his thumb toyed with my clit in those feather-light touches. My hips bucked back against his in a remembered rhythm.

"My dirty girl, ride my finger until you come."

At his words, my inner muscles clenched and I came so rapidly I wasn't sure whether it was him or me who made the orgasm happen. My hips bucked back and forth chasing more pleasure, more contact, more Marco. The orgasm should have satisfied me, but it didn't.

He added another finger and pumped into my still quivering insides. My legs shook, how I was still standing was anyone's guess. I peered down at his hand inside my panties. He saw my look.

"You want to watch?"

I nodded.

He slid his hand from my panties. My insides wept at the loss. He eased my panties from my hips, squatted once more, and eased them from my feet. Then he unclipped my bra leaving me naked while he was still dressed.

"Doesn't seem fair you still have your clothes on."

"Nothing fair about this." He shuffled me back toward the bed, picked up one of my legs, and placed my foot on the mattress, leaving my legs spread and on view to the camera. "Keep them open."

A shiver of need rippled through me. What was it about him being demanding that made me hot?

"What are you going to do?"

"Whatever I want, wife. You're mine for the night."

My insides clenched.

"You like the sound of being mine or me doing whatever I want?"

I kept my mouth shut because it was both, but I couldn't admit I wanted to be his in every way possible.

He sat on the bed and traced a hand along my inner thigh inching closer to where I wanted him most.

"Your pretty pink pussy is begging me to fill it." He spread my folds exposing me even more. "Why couldn't you have asked me before now? Hmm? You want me, don't you?"

"Yes," I panted.

"Good girl," he said, then swiped his tongue in one long lick from the bottom of my slit to my throbbing clit.

"Oh God," I cried out.

"Not quite." He smirked and plunged one finger inside me while keeping me spread open with his other hand. "You're tight, Kennedy."

"Revirginized after too long?"

He chuckled and added another finger. I stared at the sight of his two fingers pumping in and out of me at a lazy pace. Everything ached in a good way. He kissed the side of my hip. My body jerked at the unexpected arousal from something as simple as a kiss.

"You haven't kissed me since the ceremony," I said, my hips rocking with his fingers.

He gazed up at me, a flicker of emotion passed over his face, then he tugged me onto his lap and kissed me with so much hard passion my head reeled. His tongue thrust into my mouth making me groan long and deep. He added another finger deep inside, forcing me to the extremes of pleasure before the bite of pain.

"Stop." I gasped and scrambled off his lap.

He let me go and leaned back on the bed with a hooded expression.

"Come here." He crooked his finger. "Let me kiss you better."

"I ... ah..."

It was the kissing that freaked me out, not the way he'd filled me with his fingers. The intimacy, my feelings for Marco, it'd been too much in the moment.

He stood and stared at me while undressing. With each piece of clothing he removed, my mouth watered, and every other part of me wept with the need to have this man as my husband in all ways. He lay on the bed with his head at the foot.

"Sit on my face," he said in that deep husky tone that had me jumping with need.

I scrambled onto the bed eager to do whatever he

said.

"Not like that," he said. "I want your ass at the camera, and your lips on my cock."

My heart hammered inside my chest. I'd get to taste him too, have his throbbing erection in the heat of my mouth. I spun around and climbed over his face with more eagerness to give him pleasure than I was for Marco to give me more ecstasy. He spread my ass cheeks. I stroked my tongue along his length in response. His cock twitched. I wrapped a hand around him and slid his length into my mouth.

"Your mouth feels good."

I hummed in response since talking would mean I'd have to take my mouth off him, and there was no way I'd let him go now I at long last had a taste of him. His fingers massaged my ass cheeks, but he didn't lick me. I was almost glad I could concentrate on him. I licked and sucked his cock like it was the best thing I'd ever tasted, and he was. His thumbs swept closer to my ass with each stroke until sparks of forbidden desire skated up my spine. His tongue circled the tight ring of my anus.

My body jolted forward at the unprecedented pleasure, but he grabbed my hips and dragged my ass back to his mouth. He licked my tight ring again and again until my clit throbbed for some of the same attention. Anything that would make me come. He thrust two fingers inside my pussy, pressed down on my front wall and I came all over his face rolling back into his tongue as he fluttered it in time to my quivering muscles. I released his cock from my mouth to breathe and sagged against his body.

He flipped me off onto my side, lifted my leg over his hip, and slammed his cock home. For that's what it felt like. He was home. My back arched, the orgasm which satisfied me beyond anything I'd ever experienced, roared back to life with him buried deep. He thrust his cock over my sensitive flesh in the same slow way he'd pumped his fingers inside me. Every nerve ending sparked to life with each drag of his cock. His fingers brushed feather-light strokes over my clit until stars danced behind my eyelids. Any chance I'd been too tight or not ready for him was long gone. I was ready for this.

Marco kissed the back of my neck, his lips and tongue finding the sweet spot making my muscles clench around him. He zeroed in on the spot until I gasped for air, for release, for him to always do this to me. With me.

"Marco," I cried out as another orgasm claimed me, this one even better than the previous two because I had him, all of him, buried inside of me. My husband. And I loved it. Loved him.

He kept his pace slow and steady until my muscles stopped shaking, then he flipped me onto my stomach and pounded into me like he couldn't control himself any longer. I loved it even more. He came with a grunt. His pulsing release filled my overstimulated body until tiny tears gathered in the corner of my eyes.

Marco kissed my shoulder, pulled out, and rolled me over. He took one glimpse at my face and gathered me into his arms. I snuggled into his embrace and placed my head on his chest, happy to hear his heart was racing as much as mine.

"That was epic," I whispered.

He ran a hand through my hair. "Go to sleep."

"I'm not tired." I placed my lips on his chest and kissed his sweaty skin. Even the salty taste of his sweat turned me on.

"Me either," he said, tugging my hair until I looked up at him. "Are you sore?"

I shook my head.

"Good." He rolled me onto my back. "You won't be getting any sleep tonight."

"I'm good with that." I grinned.

"Bad, bad girl," he said in his husky voice.

A shiver raced through my body. How was I going to live with this being our one night together in bed? Should I change my mind? If I did, would my heart cope with it?

Marco's mouth sucked my nipple. Who cared about tomorrow when we had tonight?

Apparently, *I* did.

## Chapter Eighteen

Marco and I spent all night pleasuring each other in many ways and positions. Some I'd never even heard of before. Things I'd never even imagined doing until him.

He drove us home to his apartment first thing in the morning after we'd watched the sunrise during another round of sex. Now I was sore. I walked with short steps so as not to strain my overworked muscles into his apartment, and stood inside the front door wrapping my arms around my waist.

What the hell did we do now?

Now there wouldn't be sex unless I asked him for it, and I wasn't sure my heart would handle more sex with him. Or my body. Today at least. Tomorrow it'd be raring to go.

"Um, where are my things?"

"In our bedroom, of course." He tossed his keys in the dish on the hallway table.

"So, we're…?"

"Sharing a bed?" He raised an eyebrow. "Yes, you're my wife."

"I wasn't sure…"

"Kennedy," he said, "we're living as a married couple, and we need to act like one."

"Right." Back to the reason for this marriage. "Married people who don't have sex."

"That's your choice." He clenched his jaw.

What was he tense about?

"Yes, it is, maybe we could…?" I eased onto the lounge and winced the second my overused lady bits hit the surface.

Marco frowned. "Are you sore?"

I firmed my lips.

"Kennedy," he snapped.

"A little."

He sighed. "I should have known better than to let you convince me that last time."

I twirled my hair around my finger. "The one against the window watching the sunrise?"

His lips twitched and his gaze heated as he gazed at me. "It was quite a view."

I folded my arms and huffed. It wasn't the view which I'd enjoyed.

"Go have a bath."

"You could join me?"

He shook his head. "Water and a sore pussy do not mix."

"And you know this how?" I stood with another wince. He was right. I wasn't in any shape for more sex, and then there was the whole dilemma of my feelings. If we enjoyed sex all the time, then he'd figure out how I felt about him. "Last time I looked you didn't have a vagina."

He rolled his eyes. "I'm older than you, I know a lot of things."

"Whore." I coughed.

He grabbed my arm. "I've had a few sexual partners, but I'm not a man whore."

"Right," I drawled. "What about your video collection?"

"They are of four different women, that's all. Five including you now." He rubbed a thumb over my inner arm. "What about you?"

"Me? I … ah … I've had sex with three men including you." I wriggled in his grasp.

"Three? That's it?" His eyebrows hit his hair. "Shit."

"What about you?"

He lifted his gaze to the ceiling for a minute then said, "About a dozen."

"About? You don't even know, do you?"

"I do, but there are some you might not consider sex, more sexual encounters."

"Tomato, tomatoes," I said. "Shit, do I need to get tested now since we didn't use protection?"

He scowled. "No, you don't. I get tested regularly, and I haven't been with anyone since my last test."

"Good to know. Afterward." I wrenched my arm out of his grasp. "You know what, let's stick to the 'no sex' negotiation."

His scowl deepened.

"I'm going to have a bath now." I stomped down the hallway to his bedroom.

"Kennedy," he called out. "Don't bother unpacking, we get the keys to the house tomorrow."

Right, another thing I had no say in as his wife. I slammed the bathroom door shut childishly because he purchased a house where I wanted. It still would have been nice to be asked. It'd be nice if *he* asked *me* for sex. I ran the taps and filled the enormous bathtub with water and poured in a small dose of bath salts from the cupboard. While waiting for the tub to fill, I rummaged through every cabinet in the bathroom in a nosy way. I stripped off my clothes and sunk into the warm water. I hissed as the water hit my well-used bits. It'd been worth it, though. I'd never enjoyed as many orgasms as I'd had with Marco. My husband possessed mad skills in the bedroom. If we married for the right reasons, I'd be the luckiest woman alive.

Boo for me we weren't.

I sunk in the water until my head bobbed above the surface and closed my eyes. Besides my bits, muscles

I hadn't used in forever ached. The bath was good, relaxing, soothing.

**** 

I must have dozed off, because a hard male body was under my head and crowded along my back, thick thighs cocooned mine in the bath. A warm sleepy haze filled my body and mind. I blinked rapidly trying to come to my senses. I stirred in Marco's arms. Against his body.

"I thought it safest to support your head while you slept in the bath."

"Thanks," I said, my voice coming out raspy with sleep and arousal at having him hold me. All the remembered touches and orgasms from last night were foremost in my mind.

"It's dangerous to sleep in the bath."

"I didn't mean to fall asleep."

"We didn't get any last night." He stroked a hand up my arm.

My skin exploded with goose bumps. I sat up with a jerk. This was too intimate. Too much like something a couple in love would do. I climbed out of the bath and wrapped a thick towel around my body. His hooded gaze watched my every move as I made my way over to the sink and brushed my teeth, then my damp hair. In the mirror, I watched him as he yanked the plug and stood. His erection bobbed damp with moisture reminding me of the way he'd glistened with my arousal last night. Of the way he'd felt inside me getting coated in said arousal. My insides clamped with the need to have him again.

I spun and raced out of the bathroom and into the bedroom. Tearing open my overnight bag from our wedding night, I put on the ivory silk negligee and matching gown I hadn't the chance to put on last night.

Part of me hoped Marco liked the outfit and would have sex with me without me asking.

He walked out of the bathroom with a matching towel wrapped around his waist doing nothing to hide his arousal.

"What are you wearing?"

"Like it?" I ran a hand down the robe. "It was for last night, but I didn't get to wear it."

He frowned. "It's midday."

I shrugged. "So it's our honeymoon. Isn't this what I'm supposed to do? Lounge around in lingerie waiting for my husband to have sex with me?"

He shook his head and wrenched on a pair of gray sweats. No underwear. My pulse skyrocketed.

"You'll be waiting a long time."

My shoulders sagged. Guess he put me in my place. Marco didn't care about me or having sex with me. It'd simply been about one night for him. A way to consummate the marriage. He would never care about me. He'd made his feelings about love clear before I signed the prenuptial agreement. My poor heart chipped a fraction.

"I'm hungry. What's for lunch?" I asked.

"What would you like?"

"Food."

He rolled his eyes. "Since we can't go out with you dressed like that, I guess I can cook."

"You cook?"

"Yes, I cook. I'm not an invalid."

"I assumed rich people kept cooks, like Prue and William."

"We do."

"So where's yours?"

"I gave him the weekend off so we could be alone."

"Aww, that'd be sweet if we were an actual couple." I sashayed toward the door and peered over my shoulder. "What are you cooking for me, husband?"

"Hell if I know," he said, following me out of the bedroom and into the kitchen.

He opened the fridge and produced a carton of eggs. "How about an egg white omelet?"

"Sure, whatever. Feed me."

He picked me up and placed me on the countertop. Another wince wrinkled my nose.

"You need to take better care of yourself, wife. I won't tolerate you being in pain."

The pain in my lady bits was nothing compared to the ache in my heart. He was the reason for both of them. What would he say if I told him I possessed feelings for him and they were hurting me?

"It wasn't for no reason." I leaned back on my arms. Best to keep my feelings to myself. He'd said this marriage wouldn't be about love. If he didn't have feelings for me too it would not only make living with him awkward, but it would also shatter the hope for love I held in my heart. "It was a very pleasurable reason."

He set to work cooking, and the man grew sexier still, even more now I knew how many orgasms he could produce from my body. Orgasms I wouldn't get to experience again. Being married to Marco would suck in ways I'd never imagined when I'd agreed to this.

## Chapter Nineteen

"You have the well sexed-up glow," Prue said the second I walked into her house the next morning.

A scalding heat worked its way up my neck to my cheeks.

"Good for you." She flung her handbag over her shoulder. "I want to hear all about it tonight, but I need to scoot, otherwise I'll miss my early morning appointment. Ugh, why do rich people insist on making appointments that suit them?"

I laughed. Didn't she realize she was rich now too?

"The boys are still in bed. Bye."

I waggled my fingers as she disappeared out of the kitchen door and climbed into the backseat of the Mercedes. Gabe shut the door and waved my way. I waved back. Everyone here was like one big happy family. I was lucky to be included and now I'd married Marco I'd always be a part of their extended family, even after the twins grew up and didn't need a nanny anymore. Whatever I did to keep them all in my life was worth it.

After making coffee, I wandered upstairs, stared into my old bedroom, and nostalgia swamped me. But the new stage in my life would work out. I'd have to make it. Maybe I could be the perfect wife? And convince Marco our marriage could be more than convenience for him. It sure wasn't convenient for me. Never would be. Especially with the way I felt about him. Or the way he made me feel when he touched me. Even now, my body hungered for his and he wasn't anywhere near me.

I had it bad.

So bad. I was his dirty girl. Perhaps I could convince him how dirty I was? Last night, lying in bed next to Marco in my sexy lingerie, I'd been sure he'd crack into giving me sex. But no, he'd left me alone, cold and wanting on my side of the bed. At some stage, during the night we'd ended up spooning. I'd woken to his hard cock pressing into my backside, but again, he'd denied the need of his body, had dressed and left for work with a muttered message about picking me up from the Burberry's at five o'clock to take me to our new house.

I walked to the landing and peered out the window. Which house was it? The one on the left or right? They were both spectacular mansions. But I preferred the one on the left if I was being honest. The mansion boasted a crisp white facade with black wrought-iron balconies and a fountain in the front yard. The pool out back was almost as good as Prue and William's.

Little footsteps and tiny giggles dragged me from my daydream.

"Hey, boys. About time you sleepyheads woke up." I crouched down to their level. "What should we do today?"

Whit rubbed his eyes and yawned. "Play."

"Play what?"

"Trains," Tuck said.

"Excellent idea." I stood and herded them back to their rooms. "How about you get dressed and have breakfast first. Then we can play trains."

"Yay." They bounded back into their rooms.

I smiled. Nothing had changed between me and the twins since I moved out and I intended to keep it that way.

****

"Hey, boys." Prue wandered into the toy room and squatted at our train set.

We'd made the longest track yet, and the toys

stretched from one end of the room to the other. It'd taken us all morning to set it up and once we had, the boys lost interest. So I'd taken them to a train station, and we'd watched the trains for an hour eating popcorn like we were watching a movie. It'd refreshed them and we'd come home and played with the toy trains all afternoon.

"Mommy."

They clambered over to Prue knocking over trains in their hurry. Prue squeezed them in tight hugs and peppered kisses on their faces.

"Wow, these train tracks are amazing."

The twins showed her train after train. Prue gushed over each offering like it was the best thing ever. How she thought she wasn't an exemplary mother was beyond me. She tried hard with her kids. A lump formed in my throat. Prue noticed my expression and squeezed my hand.

The boys settled back to playing with the trains on the tracks. I stretched my legs out in front of me and shifted my numb bottom on the floor, thankful I wasn't too sore I'd wince anymore.

"So, Mrs. Lawrence, how was your wedding night?" Prue waggled her eyebrows.

I shot a panicked glance at the kids and said a simple, "Good."

Prue sighed. "Just good?"

A smile tugged at my lips. "Better than good. Exceptional."

Prue grinned. "My wedding night was the same."

My phone pinged with a message.

"Marco is here already." I tucked my legs back under me. "He bought us a house."

"Already? I don't want you moving away."

"That's the best bit. It's next door." I stood and wiped my hands on the back of my jeans.

"No way!" She stood too. "Which one?"

"I don't know."

"Come on then, let's find out." She held her hands out for the twins. "Whit, Tuck, Uncle Marco is here."

The boys dropped their trains and grabbed her hands. Uncle Marco was one of their favorite people. We all headed down the stairs and out the front door. The twins let go of Prue's hand and ran over to Marco. He gave them both a lollypop.

"Sit on the stairs to eat those."

"We will."

They sat down on the steps and unwrapped their candy.

"Marriage looks good on you," Prue said. "Where's my lollypop?"

Marco took two more lollypops out of his pocket and handed one to Prue then me.

"Thank you," I said.

He didn't let go of mine, though, he tugged me closer and planted a sweet kiss on my lips.

"Sweeter than any candy."

"Aww, aren't you two adorable?" Prue stuck her lollypop in her mouth then mumbled, "Which house did you buy?"

Marco hooked a thumb at the house on the left. I struggled to contain my squeal of excitement.

"Thank goodness for that, those neighbors were creeping me out always peeking over our fence and watching us having sex."

A jolt of panic shot through my veins.

"You could have always stayed inside." Marco laughed.

Prue wrinkled her nose. "Where's the fun in that?"

"Indeed," he said.

"Can we go check out your house now?"

Marco nodded. "Callan should be there with the key by now."

"Goodie." Prue clapped her hands. "I don't have to worry about you moving away now."

She might have been more excited than me.

Marco slid his arm around my waist and drew me into his side. If only his affection was real. I stayed in his loving embrace like the sucker I was, eager for him to love me too. Once the kids finished eating their lollypops, we walked down Prue's driveway and up the next-door driveway. Okay, I lied, I was way more excited walking up the paved driveway to my new house. Mansion. Holy cow, this was insane.

A lime-green Lamborghini sat in the driveway. Callan paced in front of the expensive car like he couldn't stay still for a second. My mind drifted back to the drawer full of whips at his house. What other stuff did he have in those drawers? Then I thought about all the things Marco and I had done in his bedroom and heat traveled into my cheeks.

"Don't worry," Marco whispered. "They cleaned the room before Callan got home."

Slight relief, but what about the poor cleaner?

"About time," Callan said.

"Blame the women." Marco nodded at us.

Callan handed a key to Marco. "Do you have a death wish? Don't you know it's never the woman's fault?"

I grinned. Callan was smart. He may have some kinks, but didn't we all?

"This part of the mansion is the three-car garage." Callan waved his hand at the building beside the house. "Let's head inside."

We walked up the stairs leading to the double glass front doors with an ornate black wire security grill. Marco unlocked the door.

"Aren't you carrying your bride inside?" Callan asked.

Marco scooped me up into his arms before I could object and carried me into the foyer.

"Oh, wow." I gazed around the expanse of the marble foyer.

A table sat in the middle, a vase with a bunch of white flowers the centerpiece, and behind was a staircase to the second floor. To the left was a large dining room housing a black table and white chairs for a dozen people. To the right was a formal sitting room with a white sofa and olive-green throw cushions, a black coffee table, and more flowers.

"All their furniture is still here," I said.

"The house comes furnished," Callan said.

"If you don't like anything, we can hire an interior designer and change it. If you want, knock out walls too," Marco said.

"Really?"

"Whatever you want, Kennedy."

Callan led us on a tour of the mansion. There were too many rooms for the two of us. A pang of longing settled in my stomach. A place like this would be perfect for raising children, but with both of us having fertility issues they were a long shot. Besides, did I want to have kids with a man I had feelings for who didn't return those feelings? That would make things even harder for me.

The mansion had a home theatre with two rows of black leather couches and a bar. There was another lounge room at the back of the house leading out to the patio through a massive sliding door. The kitchen was enormous, white cupboards and black granite countertops shiny enough I could see my face in them. Upstairs a crystal chandelier hung from the ceiling above the stairs. The master bedroom boasted a bed bigger than king size. I wouldn't even know Marco was on the other side of the bed, the mattress was that big. A walk-in robe with so many cupboards there was no way I'd fill them. The connected bathroom even held a bath. Five more bedrooms. An exercise room with a treadmill and weight set. Even a home office.

Outside was my favorite part. There was a big patch of lawn and palm trees overhanging the pool like an oasis in the middle of a desert. They reminded me so much of home that I was homesick.

The twins ran around on the lawn and all I thought about was the possibility of my children one day doing the same thing. Even running with Prue's children. As cousins. I swiped a hand over my eyes as tears built on the edges of my lashes.

"I almost like it more than Will's house," Prue said.

A snort-laugh escaped and cleared my tears.

"When do you move in?" she asked.

"The movers are coming Wednesday," Marco said. "Up to Kennedy if she wants to wait until then or stay here tonight."

"Wednesday is fine," I said. "All your stuff is in your apartment and mine."

"We can grab a few things and stay here tonight."

I shook my head.

"Come on, boys," Prue called. "Time to go home."

The boys ran into the house, Prue trailed after them.

"What about Kennedy?" Whit asked.

"She's staying here," Prue said. "Remember I said she wasn't sleeping in the same house as us anymore."

"But I want Kennedy to feed me spaghetti," Tuck said.

Another pang of regret slammed into me. I wandered over to the edge of the pool and stared into the depths of the blue water. Somewhere behind me, Marco and Callan talked, their voices like the distant rumble of thunder. They were there but not within the vicinity of my needing to know.

The squeal of the Lamborghini roared out of our new home. Marco watched me with a puzzled expression.

"I thought you'd like the house," he said.

"I do," I said, squeezing my hands together in front of me.

"Then what's wrong?"

"It's all a little too much. The place is massive, and it's only us, I don't want to clean this mansion." I forced out a laugh.

"You won't need to. We'll hire a cleaner." He shoved his hands into his pants pockets. "You wanted to be close to Prue."

"What she said … about her neighbors … it's why we're here in the first place."

"Ah."

"If she found out I watched them too, she'd hate me."

"Prue loves you. She wouldn't hate you no matter what you did."

If Prue loved me, why didn't he?

"How can you be sure?" I asked instead of the other question burning a hole in my heart.

He took his hands out of his pockets and walked

over to me. He tilted my chin up and peered into my eyes.

"I'm sure," his voice lowered to that deep husky tone that sent my pulse pounding with need.

I wet my lips. "How did you buy this place anyway?"

His lips twitched. "I negotiated with them."

"Is that your way of saying you blackmailed them too?"

"Oh, little wife, what do you think?"

"I think you'd do anything to get what you want."

His lips spread into a grin. "And they say being married is hard work. Not when your wife understands you."

I understood all too well that I wouldn't be anything more to Marco than the wife he'd blackmailed into taking his name. The wife he wanted to parade in front of his family and friends as if we were the perfect couple. The same wife he'd pleasured all night until I could scarcely move. And the wife whose love he'd never return.

## Chapter Twenty

Marco was happy on the drive back to his apartment. He chatted nonstop about the new house, which of his furniture he wanted to swap over, and which pieces he didn't care if they stayed. He checked with me each time he made a suggestion and I said yes to every idea.

If he asked me to bend over and offer myself to him, I'd say yes too. But I knew that wouldn't happen.

"Work was great today too." He settled on the couch and kicked his ankle up onto his knee giving me an unobstructed view of his groin.

Could he flaunt his sexiness any more?

"That's good." I perched on the edge of the couch.

"We signed all the paperwork for my partner status. They'll announce my position tomorrow in the office, but everyone already knew my promotion was coming."

"I'm glad it worked out for you."

I picked up my cell needing something to do other than sit there and stop myself from telling him how I loved him, or worse yet asking him for sex.

"Friday night we're going to a big dinner party with the firm to celebrate in style."

As if they knew any other way to celebrate. The rich liked their fancy dinners and champagne. I may even drink myself to happiness.

"What time?" I peered over my phone.

"Eight o'clock. We'll be in the new house then, so we'll have to leave a bit earlier than if we were living here."

"I'll be ready at seven. What would you like me to wear?"

He kicked his foot off his leg and leaned forward, his eyes flickering all over my face. "I'll buy you a dress."

"You don't need to do that, I'll buy one."

"No." He slid across the couch to my side. "I'll buy you a pretty cocktail dress. Leave your hair down too." He stroked his fingers through my hair, tugging the hair tie free from the ponytail in the process. "You have such pretty hair, it's a shame you tie this golden beauty up all the time."

"The twins were always grabbing the strands when they were younger, it was easier to keep my hair out of the way than pry it from their chubby fingers."

"Prue used to complain about that." He tucked the strands behind my ear.

Didn't he realize the simple stroke of his fingers through my hair made my body hungry for more?

I lifted my chin. "What would you like for dinner?"

He traced his finger along my jaw. "You don't cook for me, that wasn't part of the deal."

"I can if you'd like."

"The cook would have left us meals."

"Oh, okay. I'll go get them at least." I inched away from his touch.

"Kennedy." He grabbed my hand. "What's up?"

"Nothing," I blurted out quicker than a game show contestant with an answer.

"Mmm-hmm."

I jumped up from the couch.

"Next you'll say you're fine?"

"Well, I am fine," I tossed over my shoulder and strode into the kitchen to see about our dinner.

He followed me. Of course he did. I don't know why that surprised me.

"I thought I said no lies." He placed his hands on the countertop and watched me from the other side.

"I'm not lying."

"For Christ's sake, I know this marriage isn't what you wanted, but I'm trying to make it good for you." He blew out a breath. "Meet me halfway."

Removing the dishes from the oven, I set them on the counter and said, "I'm trying too." I shook off the oven mitts. "This is an adjustment."

He sighed. "I know."

Then he ate a forkful of food. Guess we were eating in the kitchen. I picked up my fork, herbs and spices drifted from the steaming dish, and I ate too. The meal was good.

"How was your day with the boys?" he asked.

I launched into a description of our day that lasted until we'd both finished our meals. Marco smiled and laughed and listened to every word as though I was talking about our children. It took little for me to imagine I was regaling my husband about our kids' daily antics. Another pang flared in my chest. I placed the plates in the dishwasher.

"I'm going to have a bath then read in bed for a bit. What do you usually do at night?"

"If I'm not working, I watch television."

"Okay, I guess I might see you when you come to bed?"

"I have a bit of work."

"Maybe not, then." I walked out of the kitchen.

"Kennedy, don't fall asleep in the tub again, otherwise you'll force me to remind you to take better care of yourself," he said in that husky tone that made me quiver for more.

**** 

I'd given up on the bath after half an hour. All I'd

thought about was Marco sitting behind me—his firm chest, strong thighs, hard erection. My body hummed with need. I'd taken to tossing in bed, the book a mild distraction from the warm moisture building between my legs.

I thumped the mattress.

This was ridiculous. Since when did I obsess over sex this much?

Since my husband gave me many multiple orgasms in one night.

The noise of the television traveled down the hallway from the lounge room. Now I'd have to get to sleep with a loud TV? Wait. I sat up. The voices on the video were mine and Marco's. Oh, shit, he was watching our wedding night. My heart raced. He said he would. I didn't expect him to watch our video this soon.

My cries of ecstasy made me jealous of myself.

I shoved a hand between my legs, not surprised to find myself damp with arousal. Was this what Marco was doing? Was he stroking his erection while watching us have sex? Did he find it as erotic as me? Three minutes of well-placed touches and I came against my fingers, but the orgasm didn't ease my hunger for Marco.

It was my husband I wanted. I longed for his fingers on my heated flesh, his mouth over my hard nipples, his cock in my welcoming wetness.

I picked up his pillow and hugged the downy softness to my chest. Inhaling deep to catch the lingering expensive aftershave he wore, I closed my eyes, settled surrounded by his scent. Like this was what I'd needed all along. An orgasm and a hug.

And a good night's sleep. Wasn't that the saying? Everything appeared brighter after sleep. Because you'd been in the dark with your eyes shut and nothing but the back of your eyelids to examine. Not a pretty sight. If you'd ever rolled your eyelids back in the mirror you'd understand.

My mind was all over the place. I needed sleep. I reverted to the good old days when I couldn't sleep and counted fluffy white sheep, getting to five thousand before the bed dipped when Marco climbed in. Pretending to be asleep, I kept my eyes shut. He wriggled his pillow from my arms then circled his arm around my waist.

An involuntary sigh slipped from my throat.

"Good girl," Marco whispered.

That was all I needed to send me off to slumberland.

## Chapter Twenty-One

Tuesday arrived and went. Wednesday arrived with a flurry of activity. The packers appeared at the apartment before I'd even left and started packing Marco's belongings. The things money could buy. I hoped he'd locked up his private video collection. I knew he had, but I still worried since I was now on those videos.

And had yet to watch any of them.

The twins were as excited as me about the move. After lunch, the removalists arrived at our new house with Marco's apartment belongings. We walked next door and watched them work. Occasionally they asked me where I wanted something, and I told them where I thought the furniture should go. Like Marco's bed. I wanted that in the main bedroom. I didn't care there was another bed already in the bedroom. I wanted his bed.

More precisely, I wanted him.

I'd take what little I could have of him since I couldn't have all of him. Sure, I could ask him for sex again and he'd willingly give it to me, but he'd never share his heart with me.

Prue appeared home from work early and found us next door. She was as excited as me and the boys watching the movers carry furniture and boxes into the house. Even William arrived home early and supervised for a while. By the time the removalist finished, Marco still wasn't home. I walked into the house and surveyed the many boxes filling the rooms.

"We can help you unpack," Prue said.

"That's all right, they're coming back tomorrow to unpack."

Prue laughed. "Right, Marco's loaded."

I frowned. I'd never really considered how

wealthy Marco was. There'd been a payout clause in the prenuptial, but I hadn't paid close attention to it since money wasn't the reason I was here. It was Prue and the fact I didn't want her to find out about my Peeping Tom fetish. I vowed then and there to never watch them have sex again.

Besides, watching them didn't have the same appeal it once did since I'd experienced life-altering sex with Marco.

Think of the orgasm-wielding devil and he appears.

Marco strode through the open door, nodded at William and Prue, then planted a knee-wobbling kiss on my lips. A kiss that claimed my heart even more and left me slack-jawed staring at my new husband wishing he felt emotions for me too.

"Uncle Marco," Whit said. "We've been helping."

"I bet you have." Marco ruffled Whit's hair, oblivious to the love pounding in my heart.

"Me too," Tuck said, not to be outdone.

Marco ruffled Tuck's hair too.

"We'll leave you two alone," William said.

"But—" Prue said.

William shook his head.

Prue pouted then brightened. "Let's have a housewarming party Saturday night."

I scanned the house and all the packed boxes. "The place won't be ready for a party by Saturday."

"Hmm, what about a pool party at our house, then?"

"You and your pool parties," William said, circling his arms around Prue's growing waist and rubbing a hand over their baby.

"Um," I mumbled.

"Yay, pool party," the twins cheered in unison.

I laughed. "Guess we can't say no now."

"It's a date." Prue grinned. "I'll ask Tiff, Dieter, and Dex too."

Without warning, Prue threw me into the married couple's circle of parties. It wasn't like I'd gone out to single people's parties anyway. Marco walked them out and closed the massive front door.

"Our first night in our new home. What should we do?" His voice dropped to the husky note.

My skin pebbled in goose bumps.

He stalked toward me. I couldn't move. Couldn't flee as I should.

"Unpack," I said, finding my voice.

"Shame," he said, "I hoped you'd want to watch a video with me."

"Sure, we could watch television … oh, you mean…" My face heated. "I don't know if I can watch myself."

"You should." He tugged the band holding my ponytail free from my hair. "You're stunning, and the sexiest woman I've ever taped."

I puffed out a laugh. "I doubt that, but thank you for saying it."

"Give yourself and me more credit, Kennedy. I may be an asshole, but I'm not a liar."

I squeezed his hand. "No, you're not." I plucked my hair tie from his fingers, turned, and made my way to the stairs. At the bottom step, I paused. "The tapes are in the box in the spare bedroom next to ours. I thought it'd be better to not have them downstairs in the theatre room."

Marco chuckled. "I suppose that's a good idea, we wouldn't want anyone putting them on to watch." His eyes sparkled with amusement.

My blush returned with extra heat. I couldn't even bring myself to watch them, let alone think about someone else watching me and Marco have sex by mistake. A part of me cringed while the other part heated.

Once again, I'd go to bed while my husband watched our wedding sex tape alone. What would he do if I joined him? Would he want to have sex with me? Or was he still waiting for me to ask him? Because each day that passed by without him touching me, my restraint was wavering. No doubt he knew it too and was waiting me out.

I sighed. He'd get what he wanted, but I'd drag it out as long as possible. If only to protect my heart a little longer.

\*\*\*\*

The next day at work—not that I'd call being a nanny to the twins work, I loved them too much—my phone buzzed with a call.

"Mrs. Lawrence?"

"Yes."

That was strange to hear. To think. I married Marco.

"This is Fifi. Mr. Lawrence hired me to unpack your belongings, I can't get ahold of him, and he gave me your number so…"

"What is it?"

*Had she found the videos? Or my box of sex toys?*

"My dad had a heart attack." She sniffed. "I need to leave."

"Of course, go," I said. "Don't worry about our stuff."

"Thank you so much, and I'm sorry."

"Stop apologizing and get to the hospital."

We hung up at the same time.

"Boys, do you want to go next door to mine and Uncle Marco's new house?"

"Can we take our toys?" Tuck asked.

"Sure can. How about we pack a bag of toys and we go play in the new house for a bit?"

They loved the idea and piled their toy cars into a bag. We walked next door; it was handy living close to Prue. This was more perfect than if I'd chosen a house for me. Marco had done everything he could to make this transition good for me too. Maybe I should stop driving him away? I surveyed the bottom floor with half the boxes unpacked.

"Okay, let's play in the dining room." I dragged the chairs out from the table, ran upstairs, and trotted back with a blanket. "Who wants to hide in a blanket fort?"

"Me!" they yelled.

The boys disappeared under the blanket with their toys and played in their happy, easy way of keeping each other amused while I unpacked the boxes. The boys thought the day was one big adventure after another as we shuffled from room to room downstairs. I took them back home at five o'clock, a second before Gabe drove Prue home. The twins told her about their day and guilt swirled in my stomach I hadn't asked Prue first before taking them to my house.

"I hope you don't mind."

"Of course not," Prue said, swinging hands with the twins. "I hope your home will always be open to them."

"It will." I loved those kids way too much. "We could turn one of the upstairs bedrooms into a room for them and they can come for sleepovers?"

"I love the idea! You're the best, Kennedy."

A smile sprung to my lips without thought. "I'll

see you all tomorrow."

Prue shook her head. "It's still strange you not living with us."

"It is." I walked back down the driveway waving at the boys.

They waved back then raced into their house. Life sure had changed in a short time. I walked back home. To mine and Marco's mansion. Already the house was feeling like home. I bound up the stairs to our bedroom. Time to unpack our clothes. I fiddled with the speaker system and put on the latest pop hits, dancing to the music as I placed my meager clothes in the expanse of the wardrobe then progressed onto Marco's shirts and suits.

"You look happy," Marco said from behind me.

I screamed and dropped the hanger in my hand.

He chuckled, bent to pick up the shirt at the same time as me, our hands grabbed the shirt together, and a small game of tug-of-war started as I tugged but he wouldn't let go.

"Let me take it," I said.

"If you wanted my shirt all you had to do was ask." His voice dipped into that husky tone that made my entire body stir to life.

As if his words forced me to look at him, my gaze roamed his shirt, my brain sent images of me ripping the buttons open and plastering my mouth on his firm chest. I licked my lips as my fingers became slack. Marco tossed the shirt on the hanger to the side and crushed me to him, taking my lips in a scorching kiss. *Holy cow.* I whimpered. Marco deepened the kiss, shoving me back onto the floor and pinning me beneath his hard, insistent body. I rocked my hips against his growing erection and on my aching core. He ground into me once, twice, then stopped.

His lips shifted to my neck and he whispered, "Ask me."

I froze. What was I doing? We'd never be more than this. An intense attraction might exist between us, but he would never involve his heart. I couldn't have sex with him again and not tell him I loved him.

"I can't," I whispered back.

He rose with a sigh and offered me his hand. I placed my palm in his and let him lift me to my feet.

"This wasn't how I imagined things between us," he said.

"Me either," I said, a breathy exhale leaving my mouth.

I hadn't imagined falling for Marco. Loving him. Experiencing this blinding heat whenever we were in the same room together. I blamed falling in love with him on the multiple orgasms he gave me on our wedding night. But even without those, I'd still feel this way.

He tucked a loose strand of my hair behind my ear that'd fallen out of my ponytail in our heated embrace. A shiver rippled down my spine from his innocent touch alone.

"We could be good together if you'd let us."

I smooshed my lips together to stop myself from saying yes. Because we *would* be amazing together as a real married couple. I saw that. I couldn't have picked a better husband for myself. The problem was, he didn't want to be a proper husband with actual feelings.

Marco left me in the wardrobe and walked into the bathroom. Seconds later the shower turned on. My mind pictured him naked and wet. Waiting for me to join him. Was he taking himself in hand and picturing me too?

I was jealous of his hand. It should be my hand giving him pleasure. It should be his wife.

## LOVE NEGOTIATIONS

Me.
He should love me too.

## Chapter Twenty-Two

I didn't even see Marco on Thursday. He sent me a text message late in the afternoon saying he'd be working late at the office. Whether he was avoiding me or working was the question that kept rolling through my mind. I'd tossed and turned half the night, and in the end, fallen asleep at one in the morning. When I'd woke, his side of the bed was still empty. Cold. Like he hadn't even come home at all.

Jealous thoughts were a curse. Was he in another woman's bed? Even though he'd said he'd never cheat, how long could he go without sex?

Friday passed in a blur, a good thing I found the kids easy to spend time with and required little brainpower. Prue mentioned I seemed tired but laughed it off as though Marco was keeping me awake for sex. I wish he was. My body and heart hungered for his.

I walked home, showered, and put on a robe since Marco said we were going out for dinner and he'd buy me a dress, but he wasn't home yet and there was only one hour until we needed to leave. I dried my hair and left it down then applied a soft style of makeup since Marco wanted a sweet girl-next-door-looking wife to parade in front of his work partners.

"Kennedy?" Marco called out.

"Up here," I yelled back.

His footsteps raced up the stairs.

"Sorry I'm late. Here." He thrust a garment bag at me and a shoebox. "Put these on and let's go." He tugged his tie free and unbuttoned his shirt.

I gasped the second the shirt opened and gave me a view of his chest. Marco paused, his gaze finally registering the robe. He stepped closer, tugged the tie free, and slid his hands on my waist.

"Be a good girl and get dressed." His thumbs stroked along the top of my panties. "I never would have thought I'd like this style of underwear." He tucked one thumb under the waistband.

My heart raced and my pulse pounded to where he touched me and lower still where I wanted him to touch me.

"Boy-leg," I whispered. Asking him for sex was on the tip of my tongue.

His thumb dipped lower, and he dropped a chaste kiss to my cheek. "I'll reward you later if you're a good girl tonight."

I sucked in a shuddering breath. He stepped back. My body screamed for more of his touch. With a shaking hand, I unzipped the garment bag. Inside was a demure cocktail dress in champagne lace. I dropped the robe in a hurry, eager to put on the gorgeous gown. I shimmied the dress up my legs, tucked my arms into the sleeves, and reached for the zipper, but Marco's fingers were already there zipping me up. He placed a kiss on the side of my neck. Goose bumps prickled my skin, but he stepped away. I opened the shoebox and gasped. The heels were even better than the dress and matched. I slid them onto my feet and admired the outfit in the mirror.

"Gorgeous," Marco said.

"Thank you for all this." I met his gaze in the mirror.

"No problem." He shrugged his massive shoulders, now dressed in a black dinner suit and wearing a champagne-colored tie matching my dress. "Let's go, we're going to be late and it's my party."

We walked down the stairs, my heels clicking a tune on the marble.

"And they'll cry if you're late?"

"Ha! You don't know lawyers, we never cry."

I snorted. "I'm beginning to understand them a bit."

"Like what?" He opened the front door.

I swept outside. "You're ruthless."

"And?"

He held the passenger door to the Camaro.

"Unscrupulous."

"True." He shut the door and climbed into the driver's seat. "Anything else?"

"You have an eye for detail." I pointed at his tie and then my dress.

"It's the finer points that matter."

He sped down the road. I grabbed hold of the edges of the car seat.

"Everything has to be fast."

"Not true." He threw a heated glance over my body.

My nipples pebbled into awareness. He was right, he didn't do everything fast. He'd played with me slow and screwed me slow. My insides clenched at the reminder. How would he reward me tonight? Sex? Because I desperately needed it.

We arrived at the Beverly Intercontinental, the impressive building that was soon becoming my favorite place to eat. As Marco predicted, we were late and his partners and their spouses greeted us with enthusiasm. I settled into the chair next to Marco slipping with ease into the role of his adoring new wife. I required no acting when I loved him and everything he did for me. Marco played his part too, paying me attention all night, making sure I'd enough to eat and drink, and I liked what they put in front of me. He also toyed with the ends of my hair while speaking with the others. He'd almost convinced me our marriage was real. Almost convinced me he returned my feelings. I wanted to believe it so much. To imagine our love was shared.

I enjoyed the burst of bubbles on my tongue and the sweetness of the liquid and was a little tipsy from the champagne. I guess expensive champagne was a lot better than the cheap stuff I'd drank before now. Before being a rich man's wife.

The dinner was over before I knew it and we were heading back to our house. Marco zoomed through the heavy traffic as though he was in a high-speed car chase. He parked the Camaro in the garage and helped me out of the car like a true gentleman. All night he'd been a perfect gentleman. Part of me loved it. The other part wanted him to boss me around. Be the asshole and turn me on even more.

"So was I a good girl tonight?" I asked, a little tipsy still.

"Very." He led me into our house, up the stairs, and to our bedroom. More precisely inside our massive walk-in wardrobe, up to the full-length mirror. "Put your hands on the mirror."

I frowned since he was in-between me and the mirror, but then he kneeled on the floor at my feet.

"Hands," he snapped.

I placed my hands on the cool glass, my pulse spiking at the commanding tone in his voice. He slid his hands up my legs from my ankles and then back down taking my panties with them, lifting my feet, and tossing them across the room.

"I've imagined doing this all night," he said in that husky tone.

"What?" I glanced down.

"Licking you until you come all over my face while watching yourself in the mirror."

A flood of moisture surged to my core and sent a throb of need pounding deep inside me. He lifted the skirt of my dress and ducked his head underneath along with his hands. His warm fingers urged my thighs apart and then his tongue ran over my clit in one long swipe.

"Oh God." I slammed my eyes shut.

"Keep your eyes open," he said as though he could see I'd shut them. "Watch yourself come."

I ground my teeth, there was no way he could tell. Could he? But he waited until I opened my eyes before running his tongue around my clit. My hips bucked into his face trying to get him to touch my aching clit instead of tormenting it. Round and round he traced, then dipped lower, his tongue lapping at the wetness at my entrance. My eyes sparkled back at me so intense as though someone drugged me with a special chemical. I suppose I was. Arousal whirled higher and pinged through my veins.

"Marco," I whimpered and rocked back and forth trying to get him to go a fraction higher so his tongue would tumble me over the edge.

He grabbed my hips hard, held them still then dragged his tongue up from my entrance to the sensitive bundle of nerves above. He zeroed in on my clit, each stroke of his tongue sending my blood pounding harder and faster until the eyes staring back at me blanked, then morphed as I exploded with an orgasm into starbursts. Or supernovas. He held his tongue against my clit letting each spasm roll against him and prolonging my pleasure. All the while I kept my eyes on my face in the mirror as he told me. As the last ripple of aftershock fluttered against his tongue, he kissed my lower lips, then my inner thigh, and lifted his head from under my dress.

Keeping my eyes on mine, I said, "Please, Marco, have sex with me, here, like this."

My face blazed back at me. Yes, this was what I wanted. His affection in any way he was willing to give it to me. It wasn't hard to ask for what I wanted. Why had I held out this long when my heart was already in, and my body was starving for his? He would at least fulfill one part of me. One part would be better than none. I could dream the love was there too. Maybe he'd feel it someday and return my love. Perhaps one day I'd have the strength to ask him to love me too.

He didn't say a word but shifted from in front of me to behind me, unzipped his pants, and plunged his cock into the wetness he'd created.

"Put your legs together," he commanded and placed his hands on top of mine on the mirror.

I placed my legs together and moaned. I was so full like this, claimed by his hard cock. He thrust his hips. My mouth opened as he stroked me deep inside. Slowly he thrust back and forth dragging the flared head of his cock over my post-orgasm flesh and turning me back into a quivering mass of need. Each thrust up forced me higher onto my tippy-toes even in heels. My eyelids fluttered shut.

His fingers left mine to stroke a hand over my cheek and clasp my jaw. "Watch yourself come on my cock this time."

I pushed back into him and opened my eyes. Our gazes met in the mirror. His steely gray eyes were too intense, and I wanted to imagine I saw more than was there. I wanted to see the love shining back at me. I dragged my gaze to my eyes, at least I'd see the love there.

"Is this what you wanted?" he whispered in my ear.

"Yes." I breathed out.

"Such a dirty girl liking to watch."

My insides clenched at his husky words. He dragged his cock out over the clenching of my muscles.

"You like me screwing you." He thrust back in.

"Yes," I panted.

"Let me make you feel like this all the time." His thumb ran along my bottom lip.

"Yes…" I opened my mouth and sucked his thumb. Could I be happy like this? I wouldn't know if I didn't try. We at least had to try at being a married couple. Married people enjoyed sex. Sex might make us closer. Perhaps we'd both be happier with sex in our lives?

He groaned deep in my ear. Slowed his thrusts so every nerve ending sparked with pleasure. I couldn't take anymore. A slow roll of his hips back in and I came around his cock. My teeth clamped down on his thumb. He held himself still as wave after wave of pleasure rippled through me and around him.

"You feel too good."

He pulled out all the way. My still fluttering insides cried out in protest. I may have voiced my objection too. He slammed into me so hard that my shoes flew off my heels, then he exploded deep inside me, his orgasm pulsing on my still contracting muscles. I leaned my head back unable to take the expression of love on my face any longer. He lowered his head and placed his lips over mine, and as our orgasms ended our kiss continued until my neck ached with the position.

Marco kissed his way down my neck and slid out. Wetness trickled down my thighs. He unzipped my dress, letting the garment drop to the floor, and scooped me up into his arms. He carried me to our bed, sat me on the edge, tugged off my shoes, then tucked me under the sheets. I closed my eyes against the tenderness he showed me. A minute later, he slid into bed next to me and gathered me into his arms. Naked. We both were. I buried my face into his chest and inhaled his expensive aftershave.

"Why did you need me to ask for sex?" I asked, tracing my fingers over his firm chest muscles.

"I'd never force a woman to have sex with me."

"Is that what you thought you did?"

He trapped my fingers under his palm against his pounding heart. "I forced you to marry me."

Did he believe he'd forced me to have sex with him on our wedding night? I'd wanted it. Longed for him. If I'd said no at any stage, he would have stopped. He might be an asshole, but he wasn't a bad man. I kissed his skin letting him know by actions rather than words that I was here by my choice, and he hadn't forced me to do anything. His hand relaxed and stroked my hair.

"I have to go to work tomorrow," he said, his voice coming out a husky whisper while his hand stroked my hair in a soothing caress.

"On a Saturday?"

"I work a lot. But I'll be back in time for Prue's pool party."

A contented sigh worked its way from my chest, and I closed my eyes. We'd have sex in our marriage. This was nice. From the mind-blowing orgasms to the cuddling afterward. We could be happy like this. Couldn't we?

It was worth finding out.

Everyone needed orgasms in their life whether or not they were self-induced. The ones Marco gave me were the best in my life. So a life full of amazing orgasms would be a good life.

"Let's have sex all the time," I said.

He chuckled, his chest bouncing under my head.

"At long last, a negotiation we both agree on."

"Hey, I've agreed on a lot of your blackmail tactics."

He rolled us over until he was on top and staring into my eyes. "Am I blackmailing you now?"

"No," I said at once.

"My good little wife." He smiled.

I smiled back. "Not all the time."

"Oh, no," he said, tracing a finger over my nipple. "You'll be my dirty girl too."

I shivered with desire even though he'd satisfied me, my body hungered for his, for his deep husky tone, for the way he made me feel about him too.

Telling him I loved him was something he'd in all probability call me a bad girl for. I wasn't sure what he'd say or do if I told him. When we'd first negotiated this marriage, he'd said love was one thing he didn't want. But it was too late now. I loved him.

## Chapter Twenty-Three

With nothing to do Saturday, since I was no longer a live-in nanny—Prue gave me the weekends off unless she and William had a business engagement—I finished unpacking all the boxes downstairs. The kitchen was now stocked and ready for Marco's cook to come back to work next week. I'd gotten used to having a cook living with the Burberrys. It sure made it easier than having to think of what to make, buy the ingredients, and then cook.

Being married to a wealthy man had its perks.

I ran on the treadmill until I'd worked up a sweat then eyed the pool with longing but opted for a shower instead.

The day dragged. I explored for more things to do and found Marco's office with a stack of boxes. I may as well unpack them too since the woman he'd hired hadn't come back, and I didn't think she would with her dad so ill. If it'd been my dad, I would have dropped everything and rushed to his side too. I couldn't fault her for putting her family first.

All the boxes held a mountain of folders. I eyed the filing cabinets. Alphabetical order seemed the most logical way to organize them. Since I'd somehow opened the "W, X, Y, Z" box, I started at the end of the alphabet and worked my way up. Familiar famous names flashed before my eyes, but I didn't dare open one folder no matter how curious I was.

Until I found one with the name Burberry.

Curiosity got the better of me. I knew about how Prue and William met when she'd worked as a waitress at a restaurant he owned, and how he'd offered her a prenuptial contract. Since a short time ago I'd signed a prenuptial contract myself, I was burning with curiosity to know what was in the Burberry's.

I bit my lip. No, I shouldn't. I lifted the file to the cabinet. My hand paused before the drawer. If the folder fell open, then it wouldn't be like I examined it on purpose, would it? I let go and the file fluttered to the floor in a disarray of papers.

"Oops," I said.

I bent and picked up the papers, they were a mess. I carried them to Marco's desk, sat down, and spread them out sorting them by page number. Wait, there were two contracts here. I needed to read each page to make sure I had the right pages in the right contracts, but with each page I read, I got more and more confused. An involuntary glower wrinkled my brow. I sat back and stared at the piles, my frown deepening.

I can't have read what I just read.

Picking up the prenuptial contract, I read the papers again. William was paying Prue for each child they had together. The baby clause didn't sit right with me. But I knew Prue, she loved those kids, she wouldn't have had them for money. Still, I was glad Marco hadn't put a baby clause in our prenuptial.

My hand shook as I picked up the other contract. I had to read it wrong. I read each word with care. Nope, I hadn't read the contract wrong.

I rammed back from the desk as though it was on fire.

Tears burned in my eyes.

Marco had a threesome with Prue and William. The words were simple. To the point and exact.

Did they love each other? Is that why he wouldn't be able to love me? I squeezed my eyes shut to stop the tears from falling. It all made sense now. Why he wanted a marriage of convenience. Why he bought a house next door to them.

I stood and ran out of the room, upstairs to our bed. I threw myself across the mattress and cried into my pillow. How stupid was I for agreeing to all this? To fall for a man who already loved not one but two people. I never would have thought they had a sexual relationship, they were close, but I'd never witnessed sexual tension between the three of them like I did between Prue and William. How did they hide their feelings so well?

Rolling over, I scrubbed my eyes and cheeks and stared at the stark white ceiling.

"Kennedy, are you ready for the pool party?" Marco called out.

I sat up with a start. Marco appeared in our bedroom. His gaze zeroed in on my face.

"Why are you crying?" He sat on the bed beside me, reaching for me.

I flinched and scurried across the bed.

"What's wrong?"

"You…" I sobbed. "Prue." I sucked in a breath. "William."

He rose an eyebrow.

How dare he act like it was nothing?

"You had sex with them," I hissed.

He sighed, tugging his tie free. "How did you find out?"

"You're not even going to deny it?"

"I'm not a liar." He shrugged out of his jacket.

"Do you love them both?" I whispered while my heart cracked.

He laughed. Of all the gall. What an asshole.

"I do, but not in the way you're thinking." He unbuttoned his shirt and stood. "William is my best friend, that's how I love him."

"But you had sex with him."

"There was no sex between William and me, I'm

not into men, so you're clear." He shrugged out of his shirt and walked into the wardrobe.

"What then?" I said, following him and standing in the doorway.

He sighed and unbuttoned his pants. "Prue wanted a threesome. William always wants to give Prue whatever she wants."

"So they wanted you? And you jumped at the chance?"

He dropped his pants, leaving me gawking at his boxer shorts. Even though he might love someone else, my body still burned for his.

"I offered." He dropped the boxer shorts and stood stark naked staring at me for a solid minute before tugging on board shorts.

I snapped my gaze from his nakedness and asked, "Why? Do you love Prue?"

"I love her for making William happy."

"That didn't answer the question." I folded my arms over my chest. "Are you in love with Prue?"

"No," he said with ease.

A relieved breath filled my lungs. "So why, then?"

He ran a hand through his hair, the first sign he wasn't enjoying this conversation.

"She's pregnant."

"So?"

"So it's not something I can do."

I snorted. "What, be pregnant? Oh, you mean to get a woman pregnant."

My heart softened a little. I understood that kind of pain. Of wanting a baby. The pain of almost having a baby then having it ripped from you and leaving you with nothing. Not even the person you thought you'd spend your life with. In a way, we'd both suffered the same loss.

"I wanted to know what it was like to be with a woman while her stomach was round carrying a baby."

"But a threesome? With your best friend and his wife?" I blew out a breath.

He shrugged. "I've had threesomes before."

"Great." I spun away. Did I know anything about him? Or his past life? Would I ever know?

"Kennedy." He placed a hand on my shoulder. "It was for one night and no more, it meant nothing between us, it was a bit of fun."

"Fun?" I shook his hand off my shoulder. "Our ideas of fun are different."

"Come on, you've enjoyed our fun."

I faced him. "That's all it'll ever be for you, isn't it?"

My phone peeled with the ringtone.

"What?" I snapped into the cell.

"Hurry up and get over here," Prue said. "The food is ready and you're late. Tell Marco to let you get out of bed." She laughed and hung up.

I tossed my phone onto the bedside table as if the device would bite me. "I can't go to the pool party."

Marco crossed his arms over his bare chest. "Put your swimsuit on and let's go."

"No." I copied him.

"Stop acting like a brat."

"Excuse me if I don't want to hang out with you and your sex buddies."

He rolled his eyes. "It was one night. It won't happen again."

"How can you say that?"

"We signed a contract."

I tensed.

His eyes narrowed. "Is that how you found out?

You've been going through my files?"

"I dropped the folder by accident." My gaze fell to the carpet. "I was trying to help by unpacking."

"You're such a terrible liar." He stepped closer. "How many other files did you snoop through?"

"None," I said.

His gaze roamed my face. "Now, *that* I believe."

"You expect me to sit next to Prue knowing you've been inside of her, knowing you both want to do it again."

"I don't want to have sex with her again."

"She's still pregnant, you know."

"I know."

"So if she wanted to have another threesome, you'd offer again."

"I wouldn't, and she wouldn't."

"How do you know? She could ask William right now for it to happen again. What if she even asked you herself?"

"Why would she ask me when she didn't even know it was me the first time?"

I gaped. "How is that even possible?"

"William blindfolded her."

I closed my eyes because I'd seen William blindfold Prue and I'd watched the sex they'd enjoyed while blindfolded. I'd also heard the orgasms she'd experienced that way too. Now all I thought about was Marco there with them.

God, I was so jealous I couldn't think straight. Jealous of everyone who'd had a piece of my husband. I was jealous he offered me the same piece of himself and nothing more.

"We're married now. I won't cheat on you."

I opened my eyes to his earnest words. They rang with truth, but the truth of his earlier words still hurt me.

Even if I hadn't fallen in love with him, they'd still hurt.

My phone rang again. I ignored it.

"We should go, otherwise she'll come looking for you."

Knowing Prue, he was right, and it'd be easier to go next door, show my face, then pretend I was sick and leave. Yes, that would work. I walked into the wardrobe and changed into my bikini, wrapping a sarong around my waist, and slipping my feet into a pair of flip-flops.

We walked next door, the tension between us like a live current ready to zap whoever touched it first. Prue smiled and waved us over. Everyone stared at us, from William to Tiff, Dex, and Dieter who all lounged beside the pool, drinks in their hands.

"Trouble with the newlyweds already?" Dex asked, a cheeky grin on his face.

"I don't feel well," I said.

"Marco, dude, go home and make your wife feel better," Dex said.

My face burned with scalding heat.

"Flowers work too," Dieter said.

Tiff grinned and snuggled into Dieter. She'd forgiven him after he'd broken her heart and they looked happy now. Could I forgive Marco for something that happened before we got married?

Prue rose from her lounger and slung an arm over my shoulders. "Ignore the men, they can be idiots. What did Marco do?"

More like who did he do. *Her.* But if what he said was true, she didn't know it.

"Nothing," I said. "I have a headache, that's all."

"Do you want me to get you painkillers?" Prue asked, the concern clear in her voice. "You've had a busy week with moving, it's no wonder you have a headache."

"Yeah, that must be it. Do you mind if I head

home and go to bed? A night of good sleep will help."

"Go on, shoo." Prue urged me back toward where we'd come from.

Marco stepped to go with me, but Prue grabbed his arm.

"Nope, you can stay here, otherwise Kennedy won't get any sleep."

Seeing her hand on his arm made me want to slap him. Not her, for some strange reason. Because she didn't know it was him in their threesome. Would she have agreed to the night if she'd known?

I hurried out of the gate.

"Prue, it's up to Marco if he wants to stay," William said.

"I'll stay for a bit," Marco said.

My heart cracked in two. He'd rather stay with them than go home with me.

## Chapter Twenty-Four

I made it inside before I crumpled into a miserable heap in the theatre room. The dark atmosphere was what my dark mood required.

Marco found me a short time later curled in a ball on the seats.

"There you are, I searched in every room for you." He stepped closer, carrying a white square box.

I tucked my legs in tighter.

"You left the contracts on my desk."

Still, I said nothing.

He sighed and sat on the other end of the long sofa. The mouthwatering aroma of baked goodness mingled with his expensive aftershave. Two of my favorite scents.

"After you left, William asked me what was wrong."

I raised my gaze to his face, ignoring the hunger pains in my stomach.

"I didn't tell him. It's the first time I haven't told my best friend my problems." He ran a hand through his hair. "It made me realize the main reason I did the threesome was for William. He's been by my side most of my life. I almost took a bullet for him in a bar fight, that's how much he means to me."

I jerked into a sitting position.

"He's always acted like it was his fault what happened to me that night." His fingers tightened on the box.

I frowned.

"When the man injured me in the tussle for the gun, he blamed himself for starting the fight. And for me ending up infertile."

I drew in a shaky breath.

"I never blamed him. It was a freak accident. It could have easily been him or the man could have shot him. He could have died."

A lump formed in my throat at the raw emotion in his voice.

"When Prue got pregnant, I saw the way he'd watched me like it was his fault I'd never have what he did. I guess perhaps I hoped after the threesome he could move past feeling like it was his fault I might never have kids."

I searched his face for the truth. Did he have a threesome to appease his friend's guilt?

He inhaled deeply, then blew his breath out through his teeth. "I'm beginning to understand now why he did it too." He slid the box toward me. "Here, this was meant to be yours anyway." He stood and turned on the television.

The cake box taunted me with its clear window. Inside sat a decadent chocolate mud cake with curls of chocolate on top. My favorite flavor.

"I don't want to watch anything with you," I said. Even after his heartrending confession, it hurt to be in the same room as him.

"You're not." He plugged a USB stick into the television. "I'm going out."

"Then why did you put the television on?"

"Because you haven't watched our wedding night yet."

I rolled my head back on my neck to face the ceiling as if that would stop me from seeing the screen. "I never want to see it."

"Or me?" he asked, his voice hoarse with emotion.

I dropped my head back down until my chin rested on my chest. The pain ripping through my body at the idea of never seeing him again hurt more than I was already hurting.

He stepped in front of me and crouched at my side. "Be a good girl, eat something even if it's not the cake, and watch our video."

I wanted to be his good girl. Desperately I wanted to be the woman he loved.

"Why?" I whispered.

He ran a hand through my hair. "You might see what I see when I watch it." He stood, hit the "play" button, and left.

Not only did he leave the room, but he left the house. His Camaro rumbled out of the driveway and down the street.

On the screen, our wedding video flickered to life. Not the type of wedding video most couples had of their wedding, but the one of our wedding night. Marco and I exploded to life on the screen. He was handsome in his tux and the way he gazed at me in my dress made me feel beautiful all over again.

My stomach made a loud grumble. I grabbed the box, opened the lid, ripped a piece off, and shoved the cake in my mouth. Damn him, the cake tasted as good as it looked. Why did he have to get my favorite food?

With each second, I watched my love for Marco grow more. As intense as the sex was in the video, Marco showered me with so much care and attention. There was more behind each touch, each stroke from both of us than the need for pleasure. The need for love and the need to return that love. With each bite of the cake, my aching heart eased. He must care about me a little to fetch me cake. Our video played all night, as we'd been in the room all night, and as the sun rose as it did on our wedding night, I saw what Marco hinted at.

Love.

My love for him shone clear in my eyes.

But there was more. The same emotion reflected in his eyes.

My heart raced. How hadn't I seen it before? Why hadn't I told him how I loved him? My legs shook, but I forced them up the stairs to my phone. I dialed Marco's number, but his cell rang out. Where was he? I glanced at the time on the clock. Barely seven o'clock on a Sunday morning. I texted Prue anyway.

Me: **Is Marco at your house?**

She'd be awake with the boys, and whatever happened between her, Marco, and William was in the past. My future depended on me putting his past discretions behind me. It wasn't like I didn't have a past. And Prue had always been there for me. She'd been a friend I needed.

I'd fallen pregnant to another man before I'd met Marco. A pregnancy that resulted in me becoming infertile too. But he didn't hold my past against me. Which he didn't have any right to anyway. I didn't have any right to hold his past against him. To stop it from us building a future. A marriage. With a bit of luck, one with love in it.

Prue messaged me back straightaway.

Prue: **No. Isn't he answering his phone?**

Me: **I want to surprise him with something.**

Prue: **I bet you do! Hang on a second.**

*Shit, where was he?*

He wouldn't be with another woman, I knew that. Marco wouldn't lie to me. He put the no-cheating clause in our contract and he wouldn't go back on it. I paced the room. My phone pinged with another message.

Prue: **William said try Callan's house.**

She sent the address next.

Callan's house. The same house we'd enjoyed

our wedding night.

I ordered an Uber and ran upstairs, threw on a dress since I was still in my bikini and sarong, then raced back down in time for the Uber.

The heavy traffic was frustrating, and out of the blue I wanted Marco's crazy driving so he'd get me through the traffic quicker. Every beat of my heart pounded with eagerness to find Marco, to talk to him. To tell him I loved him and find out if he loved me too.

I tapped the intercom buzzer for Callan's beach house.

"Hello?"

"Hi, um … this is Kennedy, Marco's wife."

Why hadn't I told the Uber to wait for me? What if Marco wasn't here?

"Hi, come on in." The buzzer wailed and the gate swung open.

I walked down the paved driveway to the beach house. Marco's Camaro sat in the driveway. Relief zinged through my veins. Callan stood at the open front door, his hands holding the top of the doorjamb like he was about to do pull-ups. If I didn't love Marco, I might have taken a moment to enjoy the bulge of his biceps, but there were only one man's muscles I wanted to admire.

"Is Marco here?" I asked, even though the sight of his car told me he was.

"Sure is." He flexed his biceps and stayed in front of the door.

"Can I see him?"

"I don't know, can you?"

"Out of the way, dick." Marco shoved past Callan.

Callan tossed his head back and laughed.

"What are you doing here, Kennedy?" Marco asked.

"I watched our video." I tucked my hair behind my ear, a slow blush creeping up my neck since Callan was still standing in the doorway watching and listening to us.

"Say thanks for letting me use your house, Callan," Callan said.

Marco threw a glower at Callan over his shoulder.

"Um, thank you." I blushed harder.

"Can you give us some privacy?" Marco asked.

"Nope. I gave you tons of privacy last time."

Marco shook his head. "You're not watching our video."

"Spoilsport, you made it in my house."

I cleared my throat.

Marco stepped closer and brushed the strands of my hair behind my ears as the ocean breeze kept ruffling the strands into my face. "He's such a dick."

"He'd have to be to be your friend." I smirked.

"She's got you there." Callan grinned.

"If you don't shut up, I'll use your whips on you."

"I didn't think you were into pain or men?" I raised a questioning eyebrow.

Callan laughed. "I like you, Kennedy, if you hadn't married Marco and your sister wasn't so hot, then we could have a real good thing."

"Sorry, Callan, but I love Marco."

"You do?" Callan asked.

Marco stopped moving, his fingers stuck in my hair.

"I do," I said, lifting my eyes to Marco's. "I know you didn't want love or ask for it. But I'm in love with you."

Marco's Adam's apple bobbed.

The sounds of the ocean echoed in the silence.

Waves slapped against the sandy beach, the call of a bird, and the swish of the breeze across the water.

"Say something, dickhead," Callan said. "When a woman tells you she loves you, say something back even if it's a thank-you."

"Thanks for your help, Callan. Now shut up," Marco ground out through his clenched jaw.

His gray eyes roamed my face.

"I'm sorry," I whispered. "I shouldn't have told you."

"No, I'm sorry," he said, dropping his hand from my hair.

My heart hurt but it wouldn't crumble. He may not return my love, but it wouldn't stop me from loving him.

He cupped my face. "I didn't want love again. The first time I loved, someone hurt me. She hurt me bad when she cheated on me. But you. You have been a pain to me every step of the way."

I frowned. Okay, this was worse than him not returning my love.

"A good pain." He stroked his thumbs along my jaw. "A pain who's made me experience things I'd never thought I'd feel again."

My aching heart eased a fraction. Did that mean he loved me too?

"What sort of things?" I asked.

"Don't make me say it."

"I'd never do what your ex-fiancée did and pretend someone else's baby was yours." I placed my hands on his shoulders. His tight muscles twitched under my palms. "I can only imagine how much that hurt. How much you wanted it to be true."

His thick lashes fluttered in a slow blink and covered the pain glistening in his eyes.

"I can't even get pregnant without you going with me to a fertility clinic."

His lashes flicked open. "If I say it, it'll break again."

"It won't." I stepped into the warmth of his body. "I'd never cheat on you."

"How do you know that for sure?"

"Because," I said, rising on my tippy-toes and touching my nose to his. "I've loved no one before you, and I never want to love anyone except you. I've never had a man treat me the way you do, give me whatever I wanted, and accept the other side of me I don't show anyone. The side that loves it when you treat me like an asshole." I touched my lips to him in a brief kiss. "Besides, no cheating was part of the negotiations. I know love wasn't part of the—"

"Screw that part of the negotiations." He slammed his lips to mine and kissed me with hunger and passion, forcing his tongue inside my mouth while his hands kept my face still for the onslaught of his desire.

A slow clap rang behind us. I flipped Callan the finger behind Marco's back. Callan laughed and Marco kept kissing me as though we didn't have an audience. As though we were the only two people in love. The only people to ever experience love.

"Why don't you two take this inside so my neighbors don't complain?" Callan asked.

Marco broke our kiss and urged me into the house. I giggled and slapped at his hands.

The scent of fresh baked goods met my hungry stomach.

"Do I smell croissants?" I asked.

"Yes," Callan said.

My stomach rumbled. Marco sighed and led me to the kitchen.

"Sit, little wife, and you can eat first."

I sat at the kitchen table. "Feed me, husband."

Marco's gaze deepened with passion. Callan placed a plate piled with croissants on the table and waved at the assortment of jams and spreads. I slathered strawberry jam on a croissant, bit into it, and sighed with pleasure. Marco shifted on the seat, his gaze dipping to my lips. I'd never seen him look at anyone like he did me. Happiness shot through my body. I loved him and he loved me.

"How is Zara?" Callan asked.

I swung his way. "If she didn't give you her number, then I'm not telling you."

A slow smile spread across his face and tugged dimples into his cheeks. "I have her number."

"She's moving here next month," Marco said.

"You don't say?" He placed his elbows on the table and chewed on a croissant.

I scowled at Callan then swung to Marco. "How do you know about Zara?"

"William told me about her being their new night nanny," Marco said.

"Another naughty nanny," Callan all but purred.

"She won't be into your kinky stuff," I said.

He chuckled. "Don't be so sure. I bet you're into Marco's kinky stuff."

"He doesn't…"

Callan raised his eyebrows.

"I don't…"

His eyebrows rose even more.

Marco laughed, deep and throaty, full of humor and happiness. I shut my mouth then burst into a giggle. He threaded his fingers through mine. A sign we were in this together. Joined in all ways. My heart warmed inside my chest. He may not have said the words he loved me, but I sensed his love in everything he did for me.

"I don't have a video camera, but you're welcome to use my sex room again," Callan said.

"You did not just call it a sex room?" I cringed.

"Why not? It's what it's for."

"We'll go home," Marco said. "I have cameras at home."

## Chapter Twenty-Five

Marco drove home like a maniac from Callan's beach house.

"Um," he said, for once sounding like me.

"What?"

"Will you be okay around Prue and William?"

"Um." I chewed my lip. I'd freaked out before thinking about it, but now after watching our video I knew what we had was more than sex. "I think so. I mean, I get you had the night before we got married and I don't have any right to be upset about it anyway."

"Are you upset about the other women I've been with, or the video we watched together of me with the other woman?"

"No." I licked my lips. "I enjoyed watching your video. Wait, do you have a video of your threesome?"

He laughed. "No."

A conflicting swirl of emotions churned my stomach. I'd watched Prue and William have sex plenty of times. I'd enjoyed watching Marco have sex. And I'd enjoyed watching us have sex.

He flicked his gaze my way. "You'd watch the video if there was."

"Well, yeah."

He smirked. "So you're not upset about our threesome, then, are you?"

I twirled my hair. "When you put it like that, then no."

"Did you enjoy watching our video?"

"I did." It turned me on every second we were on screen. Still was. I squeezed my thighs together.

"It's my favorite video." He reached across the car and placed a hand on my thigh for a few seconds before moving it back to the gear stick. "Although, every one of our videos will be my favorite."

For once I was grateful for the way he weaved through the traffic because we arrived home a lot quicker than it'd taken me in the Uber. He parked in the garage and shut off the engine. The whir of the electric garage door closing behind us sent my excitement higher that I thought I might pass out. He opened the passenger door and helped me out of the car. I took a step, but he grabbed my wrist and tugged me into his chest.

"Where are you going?"

"Inside." I wet my lips. "Where you said you keep your cameras. Let's make more of your favorite videos."

He nodded up at the ceiling. "We have one right here."

I glanced up at the small black dome security camera.

"But won't other people see it?"

"No." He backed me toward the hood of the car. "It's a private system."

"Oh," I said as he lifted me onto the warm hood of the Camaro.

He unbuckled his belt and fisted his erection. "I've been hard since you said you love me."

"Is that right?" I placed a hand over his, fascinated by the way he worked himself hard and fast. "Why don't you have sex with me like this?"

"Is that what you want?"

I nodded.

He slid his hand out from under mine, leaving my hand on his firm flesh. Hot and hard. Insistent. All mine. He reached under my dress and tugged my damp panties free, tucking them into the top of my dress between my breasts.

"This way I can smell your desire too." He

yanked my hips to the edge of the hood and nudged my entrance with his cock.

I rubbed his tip over my clit then released my hold on his cock even though I could touch him all day and never tire of it. He didn't wait, he slammed into me making my entire body shudder. I wrapped my ankles around his waist and fisted his shirt with my fingers, holding on as he pounded into me like a man possessed or racing me to the finish line. Nothing at all like our other encounters. But this one here had me sprinting with him with every hard pound of his cock. My spine arched off the hood, he placed his hands behind my back and dragged me up a fraction, pumping his cock at a new angle that sparked pleasure deep inside me.

"Oh God," I cried.

"Marco." He chuckled.

"Husband," I said.

He fucked me harder.

"Yes," I yelled and came hard and fast, stars flickering in my vision.

Marco kept going. "Say it again," he ground out.

"Husband." I tugged him to me and kissed him.

He groaned into my mouth, his orgasm claiming him the way my tongue claimed him. I shuddered against his body. He drew me into his arms and stroked my hair, kissing the top of my head.

"I love you," I whispered.

Every muscle in his body relaxed. He buried his face into my hair and whispered, "I love you too."

I ran a hand through his hair. "That wasn't so bad saying it, was it?"

"No."

"Although," I said, relaxing my legs from around his waist. "I think we need to renegotiate."

He shifted out of my arms and zipped up his

pants.

I jumped off the hood of his Camaro with a smirk.

"Renegotiate what?"

"Well, you didn't call me a good girl or dirty girl right now. We need to add that to our contract."

His lips stretched into a grin, and he crooked a finger at me. "Come here, my good girl."

I took one step closer as a shiver of desire raced through me. He cupped my ass cheeks and hauled me closer until our bodies merged.

"You dirty girl, with your panties hanging around your neck teasing me into wanting to taste you."

A new flood of arousal gushed between my legs.

"Follow me." He released me and strode toward the garage door leading into the house.

I trotted after him eager for whatever he wanted to do with me, to me, and for me. For us. Because loving my husband was the best decision of my life. Along with being his dirty girl and good girl. He'd make me feel good about my needs in every way possible because he loved me too.

**The End**

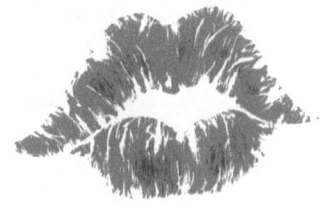

**EVERNIGHT PUBLISHING ®**

www.evernightpublishing.com

www.ingramcontent.com/pod-product-compliance
Lightning Source LLC
Chambersburg PA
CBHW030320180626
46810CB00003B/1171